# Moments in Time

## 22 Stories

# Elise Skidmore

# Moments in Time

## 22 Stories

# Elise Skidmore

Heart Ally Books
Camano Island, Washington

Published by:
Heart Ally Books
26910 92nd Ave NW C5-406, Stanwood, WA 98292
Published on Camano Island, WA, USA
www.heartallybooks.com

ISBN-13: (epub) 978-1-63107-025-9
ISBN-13: (paperback) 978-1-63107-024-2
Library of Congress Control Number: 2018950605

1 2 3 4 5 6 7 8 9 10

# Dedication

To those who cherish all the moments in time

# Contents

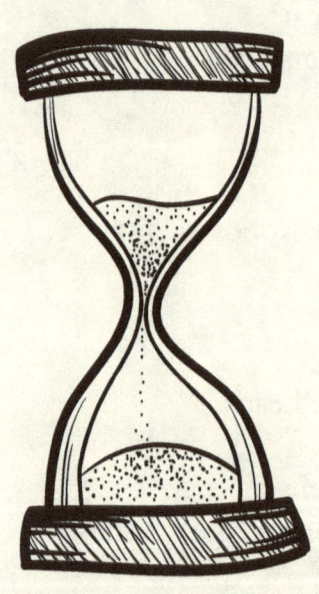

# Introduction

Every writer has their niche, the place they feel most comfortable, where they think their talents shine. For me, that has always been poetry. While I may have dabbled in essays, letters, and short stories, even as a child I was drawn to poetry, and though I rarely showed what I wrote to other people, I always had more confidence in the poetry than I did in the prose.

All that changed back in 1994 when I stumbled into CompuServe's now defunct Literary Forum and on a whim decided to try one of their writing exercises. As soon as I hit the send button, I panicked. What had I done? This place was full of real writers who were going to laugh themselves silly at this drivel I'd just posted. I was freaking out until the first responses started to come in. The people there were generous—both with their praise and their constructive feedback, and I thought maybe I can do this after all. I paid attention and kept at it, never dreaming at the time that I'd spend 10 years in that little group, even becoming a member of the staff, and offering my own brand of encouragement and constructive criticism to others.

As with any exercise, the more you practice, the better you get. I think most writers, if they're being honest, will admit that they are good at certain aspects of the job and struggle with others. I like to think I have a good grasp on character and dialog; while on the other hand, conflict is always a bit of a struggle. So while I've still not managed to complete a novel, I've written a whole lot of short stories as I keep practicing the various aspects of the craft of writing.

This anthology is a collection of some of my favorites. A couple of them have been previously published in webzines, and I've published a couple of the shorter ones on my website. They capture moments in time for a variety of characters. Some are small moments with a touch of whimsy, while others are larger, more life defining moments. There are stories that might fit in an episode of The Twilight Zone, others that may make you laugh or shed a tear. I like to think there's something for everyone. I hope you enjoy every moment.

# What's New Pussycat?

The trouble with cats is that they've got no tact.—P.G. Wodehouse

A spring breeze crept through the open window gently lifting the curtains, as the late afternoon sunlight left dappled color fluttering on the hard wood floor in a parody of Aladdin's magic carpet. At the center of this mock carpet, Harry, a large gray tiger cat, lay sprawled in his customary position, on his back with his paws stretched wide on either side. It was a crude pose, but it facilitated the act of licking his balls, which was one of Harry's favorite pastimes when not sleeping. Felix, the man who shared his home with Harry, had often remarked that had he been able to accomplish such a feat, his life would've been much easier. At the very least, he might have avoided alimony payments to four ex-wives.

Felix thought about this now as he reclined in a similar fashion on the old recliner, a glass of single malt scotch in one hand, his pipe in the other. A man had to have some consolation for the lack of feline flexibility, after all. He sipped the scotch and watched Harry's front paws swatting the air as if he dreamed of toying with a mouse. Felix smiled at the notion.

He and Harry suited each other, he mused. Their personalities were much alike; they enjoyed the simple pleasures and preferred being left to their own devices most of the time. Felix appreciated the irony of Anita (wife #4) adopting the kitten from the shelter and giving the animal a "man's" name, while he, Felix, had a name commonly associated with a cat. The fact that in time, Anita came to despise the cat as much as she despised her husband, and that she considered herself well rid of them both after the divorce was a further irony that he relished greatly.

The phone rang. Neither Felix or Harry responded to it. The cat continued chasing dream mice and Felix puffed on his pipe. The answering machine clicked on.

"You've reached Felix Granger, renowned author of four NY Times Bestsellers. Leave your number and brief message, and I'll get back to you if I feel like it."

"Felix! It's Helen. This is the fifth time in two days I've called and I'm tired of hearing that awful message! Call me back. It's important."

The shrillness of the woman's voice stirred the cat as the ringing phone had been unable to. Harry rolled to his side, giving Felix a questioning look.

"Helen," Felix said to the cat. "Wife number two. Everything's important to her. Count yourself lucky she was before your time, old man." Harry stretched, flicked his tail as if to say, "Who are you calling 'old man,' old man?" then ambled off to the kitchen. Felix downed the last of his scotch and followed him.

When he got there, Harry was waiting by the back door. Felix let the cat out and went to the refrigerator for a snack. One of the nicest things about not having a woman around the house was being able to eat whatever and whenever he felt like it. Never having to listen to lectures about how having a peanut butter, banana and chocolate syrup sandwich was going to spoil his appetite and make him fat. He slid a hand over his mostly flat stomach and scratched lightly. Felix pulled a plate out of the fridge that held the last quarter of a banana cream pie he'd bought two days ago, and supposed he was fortunate to descend from a family of beanstalks.

He sat at the table savoring the last mouthful of pie, enjoying its creamy texture and delicate sweetness on his tongue, thinking about how he didn't miss the harping and the lectures and the constant neediness of his ex-wives, but he did miss the sex. As an honest man, he had to admit the one good thing about all of his wives had been that every one of them enjoyed a good romp between the sheets as much as he did. None of them had ever cried off by claiming headaches or pretending it was their time of the month. Such a shame they weren't so accommodating outside the bedroom.

The doorbell chimed at the front of the house.

"Who could that be?" Felix glanced at his watch. Five o'clock. He hadn't been expecting anyone. "If that's some salesman or Bible-thumper come to disturb my dinner hour...."

Felix grumbled as he headed toward the front door. It didn't matter that the banana cream pie had been his dinner and whoever it was, they weren't technically disturbing his dinner. It was the principle of the thing. He flung the door open, fully intending to read the riot act to whoever was on the other side, but was brought up short when he caught sight of the stunning brunette standing on his doorstep. She wore a light blue suit that matched her eyes, with a skirt cut short enough to show off a great pair of legs.

"Felix Granger?"

Her smile dazzled him. You read about dazzling smiles—hell, he'd written a few of them himself—but they were rare in the real world. This woman actually had one and she turned it on him with full force.

His mouth went dry. So dry, in fact, that Felix thought he'd be able to spit cotton if the need arose. That image brought to mind another of Harry coughing up a hair ball and he grimaced.

The woman's smile dimmed slightly, but it didn't falter long.

"I'm Dejah Sommers." She reached out and shook Felix's hand. "It's such an honor to meet you, Mr. Granger. I've read all your books."

Ah. A fan. Well, at least she wasn't one of the overweight, suburban housewives who came up to him while he waited in line at the bank or when he was in Costco buying cat food and toilet paper.

"Thank you." He returned her smile and extricated his hand from hers. "Is there something I can do for you?" She was young enough and pretty enough that he could afford to be polite.

"I hate to intrude on your privacy, and I know it's an imposition, but I was hoping you could autograph my copies of your books for me."

She smiled again and Felix heard himself say, "No imposition at all." He opened the door wide to admit her. "Come inside, Ms. ...Sommers, was it?"

"Please, call me Dejah."

"Dejah. A lovely name, to be sure." He led her into the living room, where the scent of his cherry pipe tobacco still lingered. "Have a seat." He saw her glance at his empty glass of scotch, and added, "Would you like a drink?"

"That would be nice," she said, and Felix was surprised to see her blush.

"Scotch, all right?"

She nodded.

"Rocks? Water? Soda?"

"Whatever you're having will be fine."

He retrieved his own glass, then went to the bar. He dropped two ice cubes into his glass and filled another with ice before he poured the scotch into them.

"It's very kind of you to do this," Dejah said, as she took the drink from his hand. "You must think I'm awful, barging in on you like this. A celebrity's worst nightmare."

"You're too pretty to be anyone's nightmare." Felix smiled. "I'm curious though, how you found out where I live."

"I work in a law office, so I gets lots of practice tracking people down." Dejah crossed her legs and relaxed in the chair. Felix enjoyed the view as her skirt slid midway up her thigh. "I knew the general vicinity from the book jackets."

"Speaking of books…" Felix raised his brows inquisitively. "You said you had some for me to sign?"

Dejah reached for the soft-sided briefcase she'd been carrying and pulled out four, well-worn, paperback books, and handed them to Felix.

"I warned you I'd read them all—not just these, but all of them. I thought it would be pushing my luck if I brought more than the bestsellers though." She blushed again. Felix thought it an endearing quality.

"Just let me get my pen and we'll get started."

Felix left Dejah alone while he went to his office to find his favorite pen. On the way, he heard Harry meowing at the door. He stopped to let him in and the cat hurried past him into the house.

By the time Felix returned to the living room with pen in hand, Harry had made himself comfortable in the young woman's lap. He was on his back, as usual, and Dejah was scratching his belly.

"Sorry about that," Felix said, starting forward to take the cat.

"He's fine. Most cats stay clear of strangers in their domain, but he's just darling."

Felix shrugged and said nothing, though he thought privately that Harry was as far from "darling" as a cat could be. He opened the flap of the first book and starting signing. By the time he'd finished signing the last one, he looked up to find Harry was enjoying the belly scratch much more than was polite. He couldn't really blame the cat. Had Dejah been scratching his stomach he was sure the effect would've been the same.

"Let's trade," he said, exchanging the books for the cat, who sent him a look of the purest annoyance at being disturbed. Dejah didn't seem to be aware of the cat's arousal or emotional pique, which was probably a good thing. She was busy putting the autographed books back into her briefcase. Then she pulled an envelope out of her bag and handed it to him.

"I have something for you too."

"What's this?" Felix asked, perplexed.

"A subpoena. Your ex-wife is taking you back to court." She smiled that dazzling smile at him again. "And really, thanks so much for everything. It was a thrill for me to meet you." She turned and showed herself out.

He stood in the middle of the room, dumbstruck. Harry, on the floor and licking his balls again, stopped momentarily to shoot Felix a look that said, "At least she didn't scratch your belly first," and went back to his favorite pastime.

# The Day I Met Bootsie

I met Bootsie when I was thirteen years old. If I were Jewish, I would've been considered a man, but my family didn't have any religious ties and, even now, thirty years later, I'm still considered the baby of the family. My brother, Rob, is thirteen years older than me, and is much closer to the twins, Lance and Lindsey, who came along two years after him. None of them paid me much attention back then. I always seemed to be in their way.

Looking back, I can't say I blame them. My father ran off when my mother told him she was pregnant. Lance always said that was the reason my mother went nutso. He might be right. Something like that's bound to have an effect on you.

Ginny (she never wanted me to call her Mom) wasn't crazy enough to be in a locked room, but she took plenty of anti-depressants. They'd work for a while, then suddenly she'd flip out. Today she'd be labeled bipolar, I guess, but her highs never seemed as extreme as the lows. I tried to stay under her radar as much as possible, but I never knew when she might crash through the door and rip the posters off the wall or shred my sketchbooks in a blind rage.

In any case, it left me on my own a lot, which wasn't all that bad. It gave me plenty of time to draw and that's what I was doing the first time I saw Bootsie.

From my bedroom window I could see most of Green Street Park, and spent hours sketching anything interesting that went on below. One afternoon in late September, when the air was still warm and a steel-colored sky threatened rain, I noticed a girl strolling along the path. She had curly blonde hair and wore an azure blue polka-dotted dress with no coat. She looked very young, but that might have been because of the bright red galoshes she wore, the kind mothers force little kids to wear so they won't ruin their shoes when they run through puddles.

Anyway, I couldn't tell for sure how old she was, but something about the way she moved whispered misery, in spite of the bright colors she splashed against the gray sky. She sat down on one of the benches, folded her arms across her chest and stared at the sky, as if waiting for an answer to some important question.

When the rain started and she made no move to leave, I decided to investigate. I grabbed the big umbrella from the stand in the hall and trotted over to the park.

"Hey there, Bootsie," I said, taking a seat beside her and casually letting my umbrella protect us both. Now I could see she was a little older than I'd thought, probably around nine or ten. "Are you lost or something?"

"My name isn't Bootsie," she said, frowning. "It's Elizabeth."

"My name's Dennis, but my family calls me Denny. Denny's not nearly as cool as nickname as Bootsie though," I said, trying to make her smile.

Bootsie didn't say anything but, now with the umbrella over her, I saw that it wasn't only rain that streaked her cheeks.

"Why so sad? Are you lost?"

"No," she said, sniffing and wiping her nose with the back of her hand. "I live over there." She pointed down the street to the pretty yellow Cape Cod style house with a white picket fence. I knew it well. The old couple who lived there paid me to do yard work and shovel snow.

"You live with Ralph and Maude?"

She nodded. "They're my grandparents."

Bootsie didn't volunteer more information so I pondered that for a minute while the rain beat a solid tattoo on the umbrella, and the damp made her curls frizz. I knew the Gerbers were nice folks and wondered why staying with them made Bootsie so sad.

"So where are your parents? On vacation or something?"

"They died," she said, then doubled over sobbing, with her face pressed against her knees.

I switched the umbrella to my other hand, and patted her back gently, not knowing what to say. She sat up abruptly and pounded her fists on her knees.

"They shouldn't have left me!"

"I'm sure they didn't want to leave you. I mean, if they died, it wasn't their fault—"

"They left me all alone!"

"You not alone. You've got Ralph and Maude—and they're great people, really nice," I said, addressing the facts because I didn't know how what else to do.

"I love Grandma and Grandpa, but I miss my Mom and Dad. They shouldn't have left me. If they took me with them when they went out to dinner that night, I'd be dead too and we'd still be together."

"Don't say that."

"Why not? It's true."

"I bet your parents would be real sad if they heard you say something like that."

"What do you know about it?" The sarcastic tone would've done my brother Lance proud.

"You know, it could be worse. You're lucky—"

"How can you say that? My mom and dad are dead and I'll never see them again. Easy for you to say I'm lucky." She looked like she wanted to hit me.

"No, not easy. I mean, it's awful that your folks are dead, but they didn't have a choice. My father didn't die—he ran off when he found out my mother was pregnant with me. My whole life I've been blamed for that. I've lost count how many times I've heard, 'Everything was fine until you showed up.'"

I shook my head. "I don't know, but I think it would be easier knowing my dead parents loved me than it is knowing my parents wish I was never born."

I had thought these things many times, but had never said them aloud before. Why I said them to this sad little girl, I don't know, but that's what came out. In spite of the umbrella, my cheeks were wet too.

Before I had a chance to do anything about it, Bootsie held my face in her small hands and wiped my tears away with her thumbs in a oddly maternal gesture. I swallowed the lump that had formed in my throat and smiled at her.

"Thanks," I said.

"You're welcome." All at once, she sounded very grown up, and the expression on her face grew thoughtful.

"Want me to walk you home, Bootsie?"

"I told you, my name's Elizabeth," she said, with only mild annoyance.

I smiled at her again and glanced down at her bright red galoshes. "You'll always be Bootsie to me."

She chewed the inside of her cheek for a minute, while she studied me. "Okay. You can call me Bootsie, if I can pick a nickname for you. You're right—Denny doesn't fit you."

"What does?" I asked, amused.

She tapped a finger on her chin. "How about Elvis? You've got blue eyes like his."

I laughed. "I don't think that's quite right."

"Maybe not," she admitted. She stood up and took my hand. "I'll think about it some more."

The rain had stopped, but I let the umbrella shelter us anyway as we started toward her grandparent's house. Her hand was small, but it felt good in mine. Natural. Age doesn't matter, I thought, we're going to be friends for a long time.

She must have sensed it too, because she squeezed my hand and her smile reached her eyes this time.

"It might take me a while to come up with the just the right name, you know. Can I count on you to be around until I do?" she said, seriously.

I knew she wanted reassurance that I wouldn't be one more person who'd desert her.

"As long as it takes," I said.

We've been married for twenty years and Bootsie's still trying out nicknames.

# Edmund's Story

My name is Edmund Howard, both names derived from the old English; Edmund meaning "happy defender" and Howard, "chief guardian," both of which are invested with an irony that will become clear later on. I became what I am on a battlefield in the south of England long centuries ago. The exact date is unimportant; let it suffice to say Henry VIII had not yet begun collecting wives and be done with it. The details can be filled in with human imagination; one tale of conversion is much like another.

Anne Rice based all of her vampires on me. She took certain liberties, not the least of which was turning me into a Frenchman, but Louis, Lestat, Armand and the others were all parts of me. I was the vampire she interviewed and most of what she turned into her literary legacy has happened to me at one time, in one form or another—with the notable exception of Lestat's adventure with the Body Thief. I could never be so stupid as to fall for a trick like that one. Still, writers are expected to fabricate tales to enthrall their audience, and at least she stayed truthful on the salient bits, unlike some others I could name. While I have been able to see the sun without burning to ashes, I'm an exception, rather than the rule, and on those occasions my skin did not sparkle as if I'd been brushed with fairy dust. I am most assuredly a creature of the night, existing in the world of dark and shadows. After so many centuries, I can go for long periods of time without feeding or taking rest, but again, I am the exception which proves the rule.

Most vampires don't survive long enough to get to this point. The initial feeding frenzy abates, followed by the thrill of the hunt, which later becomes a necessary diversion, until finally ennui settles in and existence loses its appeal altogether. When that happens, one has no choice but to act foolishly, doing things that will lead to the ultimate demise. I have seen this play reenacted many times, and I think most of us would not consider it an unhappy ending. What is a life without purpose, after all?

To avoid that end, two hundred years after I became what I am—or it might have been three hundred, time is funny that way, especially when it appears it will go on forever—I challenged myself to find a hobby that would never become boring. One might wonder what would hold the interest of someone who had forever—I know I did—and after much consideration of the matter I decided to invest my energies in the ever-changing, always unique, sea of humanity. While some might argue that mankind is predictable, I have found, that taken individually, human beings hold the constant promise of surprise. Once a generation, I will seek out one who strikes me as having potential to take under my wing and I become a sort of guardian angel to them (you should pardon the expression). Thus we arrive at the irony I spoke of earlier.

It was in Brooklyn, New York, in the summer of 1969, not long after I had risen for the night, but early enough that children still played in the streets, that I first saw Francine Scanlon. She was a beautiful child on the edge of womanhood, with red hair that glittered like rubies in the reflected lamplight and the incarnadine skin of someone who had spent more time in the sun than was wise. Even from my distant observation point I could see the laughter shimmer in her green eyes as she played with a younger, less striking version of herself. She turned a rope that had one end tied to a parking meter and sang some nonsensical chant while her sister attempted to jump in time. Each time her sister faltered, Francine would encourage her to try again. Her sister had no talent for jumping rope and tripped up after two or three successes each time, but Francine had the proverbial patience of a saint and this play went on for nearly an hour until the street was full dark, when a frowzy woman stuck her head out of a second storey window and yelled for the girls to come in.

Something about Francine called to me. It may only have been her resemblance to my own long-dead daughter, Mary. She, too, had red hair and laughing green eyes, though I doubt she would ever have had Francine's forbearance in lieu of what transpired. In ancient times red hair was thought a sign of the devil, but I have always been enamored of women with red hair. Mary's mother had red hair, though it turned out she lacked the fiery spirit common to most redheads. While good-natured, even as a child Mary did not suffer fools lightly, and was just as likely to forge head first into the fray at perceived injustice as she was to look for help from other quarter, much to her mother's dismay. What can I say?

She was her father's daughter and came by her temperament honestly.

Whatever it was, I began my silent guardianship of Francine after that first sighting, watching her grow and mature from a distance. I did not interfere with her day-to-day existence, nor try to influence her in any way. My intent when adopting a new ward (for lack of a better term) has always been to observe as unobtrusively as possible. Only a very few have been aware of my existence, though they tend to credit some obtuse guardian angel with watching over them, which I find amusing or annoying, depending on my mood. Even fewer have interacted with me directly. I find it best that way. Mankind, while enjoying the literary fantasy of vampires, really doesn't want to come face-to-face with their reality. Staying in the shadows frees me from the tedium of explanations or cleaning up messy situations, and as I may have mentioned earlier, avoiding boredom is the reason I've lasted as long as I have.

Francine appeared to be doing well for herself, in spite of expectations. Her father had disappeared long before I spotted her and her mother had let his desertion drag her to quiet despair. The woman went to work to keep a roof over her daughters' heads, but she also made a habit of imbibing to excess, and it fell to Francine to become a surrogate mother to her younger sister. Francine took this all with good grace, turning down a scholarship that would have left her sister to fend for herself, and taking night courses at a local college instead.

It took her a while but she earned a nursing degree and found a job in the hospital emergency room. Though you may think me ghoulish, I delighted in her chosen profession. I reveled in the opportunity to be around the blood and found the gore fascinating, even more so, the ways modern medicine has found to heal wounds and diseases that devastated the people of my time, my time being the time before I became what I am, of course. Also, I found a certain irony in my preference for the sanguinary being linked to her choice of career, in a manner of speaking.

It was while Francine was still going to school, but not long before she got her degree, that she met Vincent Figaro. He was a policeman, impudent and bold, who brazenly accosted her on the street as she walked home one evening after class to ask her to go out with him. He was Italian, with the dark good looks and cocky self-confidence that so many women have found admirable throughout history. To my amazement, Francine agreed and it wasn't long before she and "Vinny" had set their wedding date.

I should not have been so irked by her actions; the very fact that human beings are prone to such foolishness and unpredictability is what has held my interest for so long, but I had grown fond of Francine, and Vincent had a subdued aura of violence that screamed to my senses so loudly I could not believe that Francine did not sense the contumelious nature that lurked just beneath his easy smile. They do say love is blind, so I suppose that must explain it.

It did not take long for Vincent to show his true colors. Francine's recently acquired ineptitude resulted in bruises, sprains, and the occasional black eye. If her friends and co-workers suspected her husband's perfidy, none of them ever mentioned it to her. Once her sister tried to broach the subject, but Francine managed to convince her that the bruise on her throat was the result of Vincent having had a vivid dream involving the apprehension of a particularly nasty felon, a one-time event rather than an ongoing problem.

You may be asking yourself how I come to know so many intimate details when I claim to go unnoticed (unless, of course, I choose not to). Let me say, without delving too far into particulars, that vampires have many talents that humans know nothing about, and a vampire as old as I am acquires a good many more than what is common among the general vampire populace. For example, I am capable of standing beside you without your knowing it. You might possibly sense your hackles rise or a sudden chill run up your spine—the phrase "a goose walked over my grave" comes up often in these cases, but you would have to be extremely sensitive even for that to happen—or I distracted by other things at the time. Rare, but it does happen.

In any case, even with Francine's saintly patience, I continued to be astonished—and perturbed—by her steadfast belief in her husband's love for her, and puzzled for many hours over why she stayed with him, risking her life (and later on, her child's life) to his capricious ire. Any reasonable person would have come to the conclusion that a man who abuses his wife to such a degree does not hold any true affection for her. Even before my sempiternal existence began, it was common for many men to physically punish their wives, but in that respect, I suppose, I was a man many years ahead of my time. I have always found it most distasteful to display such a lack of self control as to lay hands on women and children, just because one is capable of it.

By the time Francine had decided that enough was enough, her son was nearly ten years old. Vincent made the mistake of doing more damage to her face than could easily be explained away by walking into a door or tripping over the cat and falling into a table. Even at that, I believe what finally drove her to action was the look on her young son's face when he came home from school and saw her sitting at the kitchen table in her blood-soaked blouse with the ice pack covering half of her face. That evening while Vincent was at work, Francine called an abuse hot line and within twenty-four hours, she and her son were secreted away by a group of caring strangers in the hope of beginning a new life far from the violence and pain of the old one. They were given new names (in another ironic twist of fate, Francine became Mary), along with a source of income and a place to live a thousand miles from their home in Brooklyn.

I followed, naturally, curious to see how things would turn out. Florida was not particularly to my liking. Had I blood running through my veins, I could not have tolerated the insects, which were large and seemingly insatiable; fortunately, I do not. Francine's son was enrolled in school and she found employment as a visiting health aid, a job much beneath her nurse's status, largely consisting of checking blood pressures, changing sheets and making sure the patients had what they needed to survive until the next visit. Things were difficult, but life was improving for them. However the need to keep secreted from Vincent was a constant gremlin that niggled at Francine, who worried that with his police contacts he would somehow find them. In spite of this, by the time six months had passed, she had managed to make a few friends and slowly began the titivations that would turn their new apartment into a home.

Then came the night that Francine's worst nightmare became reality.

Her son was gone on a weekend camping trip with a friend, and she had accepted a dinner invitation from a pleasant young man, as different in appearance and temperament from her husband as a man could be. She looked exquisite in an emerald green dress that suited her natural coloring and slender figure to perfection, and a glimmer of light shone again in her eyes. It was the first time in a very long while that I had seen a resemblance to the beautiful young woman who had played jump rope in the street with her little sister. To borrow an expression that is not technically accurate, but true nonetheless, it warmed my heart to see Francine happy. Alas, this turned out to be an ephemeral pleasure for both of us.

When she returned home that night, Francine walked into her bedroom and flipped on the light to find Vincent waiting for her. He sat on her bed, smoking a cigarette, with pillows propping him against the headboard. The hand closest to the side of the bed raised a baseball bat with casual menace. He spoke to her in the voice of purest evil, usually given to characters like me in films and theatricals. "You stole my son, Francine. MY son. You shouldn't have done that. I'm going to make sure you don't ever try that again."

He rose from the bed then and the paralysis that had momentarily fallen over Francine lifted. She turned and ran, but had I not been there, it would have done her no good at all.

I let her pass me in the shadowed hall, but stepped forward when Vincent would have grabbed her by the hair. With one hand I grabbed him by the throat and held him up against the wall. His legs dangled inches from the floor and his eyes rolled wide in shock. Clearly, he wasn't used to being the one pinned to the wall. I grinned maliciously, exposing my fangs, as I repeated his earlier words to Francine. "You shouldn't have done that. I'm going to make sure you don't ever try that again." I was gratified to see the shock turn to fear.

It was quick work and the deed was done before Francine had a chance to call the police. She was frightened when she saw me carrying Vincent's carcass, but as I said earlier, I have many talents and it wasn't long before I had calmed her. Vincent would never hurt her again; he would disappear without a trace. I would take care of everything.

I used my talents to ensure that what she had seen dissolved into her subconscious mind, and only the freedom of knowing she didn't have to worry about Vincent anymore remained. Then I slipped back into my world of shadowed observation, where I remain content to watch Francine and her new family grow and thrive. I hope she lives a very long life. Even devils like a happy ending now and again.

# Clothes Make the Man

**M**ax Stratton pulled the business card from the pocket of his gray Armani suit and double-checked the address. *Clothes Make the Man, 22 Sentinel Lane.* He looked again at the narrow store front with its blackened windows and wondered how long it had been since Vivian's friend, who had recommended the costume shop, had actually shopped here.

"Trust me, Max. It's the most amazing place. The man who runs it is darling—even if he is a trifle mad. The costumes are real antiques, yet he sells them for a pittance," Natalie had said, when she slipped the small, handwritten business card into his palm.

Why the devil did Vivian have to make their New Year's party a costume ball? As if there wasn't enough craziness on New Year's eve without her adding to it! But Vivian adored playing dress up and thought it was a fabulous idea. After twenty years of marriage, Max knew better than to argue about Vivian's parties—not if he wanted any peace in the next twenty years.

But Clothes Make the Man seemed to have gone out of business. No mannequins modeling in the windows. No interior lights that Max could see. Not even a "Sorry—We're closed sign" hung in plain sight. If it wasn't for the number twenty-two painted in gold over the door frame, he would've sworn he was in the wrong place.

Annoyed at the wasted trip and wondering where he was going to find a costume now, Max shoved the business card back into his pocket and turned to leave. Just then, bells jingled behind him as the door to the shop opened.

A tiny old man in brown striped trousers with a matching vest stepped out. His white shirt with red garters holding up the sleeves, gave him the air of an aging pawnbroker. At 6'2", Max towered over him by at least a foot. The man pushed a broom with a handle almost as tall as he was, and worked with his head bent, concentrating all his energy on sweeping the dirt away from the store front. Max was a bit surprised that the man didn't even acknowledge his presence. He faked a cough to get his attention.

"Excuse me. I'm looking for a costume shop called Clothes Make the Man. This seems to be the address, but…."

"Oh, you got the right place, all right. Come in, come in," the man said, looking up from his task. He motioned Max to follow him with a grin that revealed a mouth full of crooked yellow teeth, but there was childlike enthusiasm in his voice which surprised Max.

"The name's Horace Barkley," he said as he reached out to shake Max's hand. "I'm the proprietor of this fine establishment. What can I do for you today?"

"I need something special for a costume ball my wife's throwing on New Year's Eve. Your shop came highly recommended."

"Yes, yes, we specialize in the extraordinary," Horace said with good-natured pride. He prattled on about how business had been slow and how he'd lacked the extra cash for fripperies, as he moved through the shop tugging on dangling strings connected to the overhead lamps. Dim circles of light spilled over faceless mannequins dressed in costumes dating back hundreds of years. At a glance, Max saw a colonial minuteman, a cowboy, a Roman gladiator, and what appeared to be a member of the French aristocracy from the eighteenth century, complete with powdered wig.

He moved closer, admiring the fine detail of the clothing.

"Impressive, Mr. Barkley. Everything looks so authentic."

"Oh, it's authentic, all right. Those aren't costumes, Mister… ah, what did you say your name was?"

"Stratton. Max Stratton."

"Mr. Stratton. No, sir, all my clothes are the genuine article. No reproductions."

Max raised an eyebrow. "Indeed? In that case I imagine they must be extremely expensive. No wonder business has been slow." *If he thinks he's going to make up his losses on me, he's got another thing coming,* Max thought.

"Oh, I wouldn't say that. After all, we are talking about used goods. Certainly wouldn't expect you to pay brand new prices for recycled clothing. No, sir, Mr. Stratton. That wouldn't be right."

Max's eyebrow shot up again, but in surprise rather than cynicism. "Well, how much do you charge?"

"That depends."

"On what?"

"On the clothes, of course. And whether they make the man," Horace Barkley said, scowling at what he obviously deemed a stupid question. "Look around. See what suits you. When you find something, let me know and we'll discuss price."

Max nodded his approval and began browsing the merchandise.

The store was much bigger than it appeared from the outside, with two long rows of mannequins running down the middle of its narrow length. On close inspection, the costumes did appear to be genuine antiques, like something one might find in a museum. He was certain they were worth a small fortune. Well, Natalie had said the guy was crazy.

He studied each display, eliminating several at a glance. He certainly didn't have the legs for the gladiator get-up or the highlander's kilt. And nothing in the world would get him in the minstrel's tights. Max did fancy the Louis XVI nobleman's costume with its silk brocade jacket with jeweled buttons, but it looked made for someone much smaller than he was.

"Have you seen this one, Mr. Stratton?" Horace said, pointing to a figure wearing the gray uniform of a Confederate soldier. On its head was a regulation kepi with its linen havelock draping over the neck to protect the wearer from some long ago sunburn. A bulging haversack had been slung over its shoulder and a rifle, complete with deadly looking bayonet protruding from its muzzle, leaned against the crook of the faceless mannequin's arm.

Max's face lit with interest. The uniform, bathed in a pool of dim light, beckoned to him. He'd always been a Civil War buff and here was a chance to wear a uniform that some young Johnny Reb might have worn into battle.

"It's incredible. It looks so real."

"Told you before. It is real. Right down to the underwear."

Max held his breath and reached forward with tentative fingers to remove the soldier's hat. "May I?"

"Sure, go right ahead."

Horace watched Max adjust the hat and check out his image in the full-length mirror beside the dressing room.

"Well, the hat fits," Max said, hopefully.

"Why don't you try on the rest of it? Looks like it might be the right size to me."

He nodded in giddy anticipation, wondering what the soldier who originally owned the uniform might have felt before a skirmish.

"Good. Good," Horace said, as he removed the rest of the uniform with amazing speed and nimble fingers, then ushered Max into a small dressing room. "There you go, Mr. Stratton. I have a feeling you've found something to suit you." He giggled, an odd sound coming from such an old man, then drew the curtain to assure Max's privacy as he changed clothes.

The dressing room barely had room to turn around in, but Max managed to remove his suit and hang it on one of the wall hooks. He looked at the antique garments Barkley had hung on the other hook and saw the old man hadn't been joking when he said it came complete with underwear. For a moment, Max considered leaving on his own tee-shirt and briefs, but for some reason he couldn't quite put his finger on, he decided to strip down to the buff and try on everything. In for a penny, in for a pound, he thought with dry amusement.

He fumbled with the buttons on the fly, amazed to find each one had CSA embossed on it. Must've been a real pain in the ass when you had to pee, Max thought, and made a mental note not to drink too much when he wore this to Vivian's party. That startled him because, suddenly, he knew in his gut no matter how much Barkley wanted for the uniform, he was going to have it.

Fully dressed, he stepped out of the cubicle and studied his reflection in the mirror, delighted by what he saw. The uniform fit as if it had been tailored to his exact measurements. He straightened to his full height. The trouser length was perfect and even the boots fit perfectly. Max turned to check out the side view and Horace thrust the bayoneted rifle into his hands.

"Here. You'll need this."

Max held the gun with both hands, momentarily surprised by its weight, then hefted it over his right shoulder, cupping the butt in a parade stance. He spoke down to Barkley's diminutive reflection beside him in the mirror.

"How much? For everything."

"Well, let's see," the storekeeper said, tapping his chin thoughtfully as he made mental calculations and mumbled to himself.

"Don't jerk me around, Barkley. Name your bottom price and I'll take it off your hands today."

Horace crooked his neck to peer up into Max's stern face and grinned, this time keeping his lips tight together so Max wasn't exposed to those awful teeth.

"I think thirty dollars will cover it."

"What?" Max's jaw dropped. "I must have misunderstood. I thought you just said 'thirty dollars.'"

"I did. Most of that's for the rifle which went for about twenty-five or so when it was new, but taking into account depreciation and wear and tear on the clothes…. Yes, thirty dollars should do it."

He is crazy, Max thought. "Sold." Then, before Barkley had a chance to change is mind and up the price, Max reached into the dressing room, grabbed his wallet from his own pants' pocket, and handed the old man two twenty dollar bills. Barkley headed away to the cash register to get his change and Max went back inside the cubicle. He closed the curtain with one quick pull.

In that moment, an explosion boomed outside the cubicle, its force flinging him into the wall. He smashed the side of his face on the wall hook. When he touched his cheek, his fingers were covered with blood.

"What the hell?"

He heard shouting and suddenly remembered the shopkeeper. Max stood up and reached for the curtain, calling the old man's name.

The shop had vanished behind a cloud of smoke, which filled his lungs and triggered a spasm of coughing. He smelled gun powder. Jesus, had somebody bombed the place? He covered his face with one arm and stepped further into the room. He couldn't see a thing but he heard voices, lots of them. Some were yelling, but he couldn't quite make out the words. Others were screaming, shrieking in pain. Had anyone else come into the shop when he wasn't looking? Were the shouts paramedics already on the scene?

Another explosion shook the ground. Without thinking, Max threw himself to the floor and covered his head with both arms. Something thudded to the ground next to him. He reached over to see what it was. For a moment he thought one of the mannequins had lost a leg. Then he saw the ripped flesh and the blood.

He screamed. "Hey! Somebody! Over here! I need help!"

Men were running all around him but none stopped to help. The dark was alive with sound, the loud retort of gunfire and the clanging of steel against steel. It felt like he was in a battlefield.

What the hell is going on? Max thought. He touched the sleeve of the confederate uniform he wore. It was filthy now and covered with his blood. This has got to be a dream. There's no other explanation. I banged my head in whatever that first explosion was and this is just some weird hallucination. That's got to be it. If I can just get outside and into some fresh air, I'll be all right.

Max dragged himself to his knees and started crawling in what he hoped was the direction of the exit. All his focus was on getting outside, trying desperately to ignore the sights and sounds of the battle raging all around him. He willed himself not to believe what his senses told him.

"Where do think you're going, private?" Max froze in his tracks, trapped by the commanding voice of the confederate officer standing in front of him.

"There's been some mistake—Sir," Max added hastily.

"I'd say so. You're heading in the wrong direction, private. The enemy's that way." The officer used his saber to point behind Max. "You wouldn't be trying to desert in the middle of a battle now, would you private?" The voice was low and menacing, and hallucination or not, it terrified Max.

"No, sir. I wasn't deserting. I…I…I was looking for my rifle. I lost it in the fracas."

"Take another from one of the fallen and get your ass back there. And be quick about it or I'll shoot you myself!"

"Yes, sir," Max said, then searched the ground around him for a weapon. He thought about going back toward the dressing room for the rifle with the bayonet, but he didn't know where the damn dressing room was anymore. The officer had disappeared in the smoke, probably busy fighting Yankees, Max thought.

He decided to make a run for it. He hadn't gone ten yards, when Max heard the officer's voice shouting after him. "Stop right there, you cowardly bastard."

Ahead, Max thought he saw a lighted doorway. He kept running, pushing himself as hard as he could. He felt something whiz past his ear, but he had no time to think about what it was. A little further and he knew the light was the dressing room; he could see the curtain he'd pulled back. There were more shouts but he kept his head down and sprinted forward.

Six feet from the doorway, where he could see his Armani suit hanging on the wall hook and the bayoneted rifle leaning against the wall, the bullet struck him in the back. Oh god, I'm dead, he thought, then fell, face down in the dirt.

Horace Barkley smiled as he showed the latest prospective customer his merchandise. With great pride, he informed him that each display contained authentic clothing from the time period and was not a costume. The gentleman seemed taken with a confederate uniform standing in the corner and asked the price.

"Oh, this one's slightly damaged. See," said Horace, pointing to the back of the gray coat. "There's a bullet hole tear. I suppose I could let you have it—complete with accessories, of course—for oh, say twenty-five dollars?"

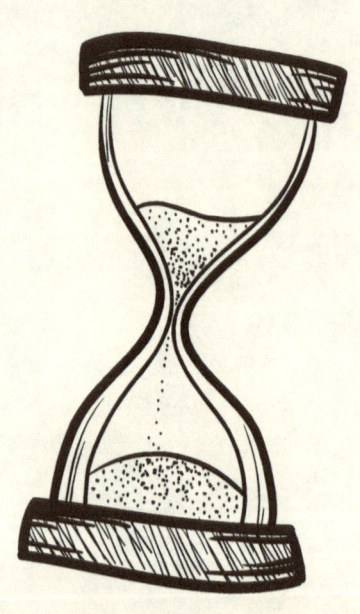

# Charades

"Yes, Mother…I know what day it is…I've turned forty, I'm not brain dead."

Arly Jackson sighed as her mother continued her nagging disguised as birthday wishes. She gripped the phone between her cheek and shoulder, freeing her hands to feed her cats. Yin and Yang, demanding as only Siamese cats can be, weaved in and out between her ankles, nearly tripping her in the process. Once their breakfast was served, Arly made her way to the living room, her mother's voice still droning in her ear.

She plopped onto the leather sofa scarcely noticing the gentle hiss as the cushions squished together under her weight. The apartment, decorated solely in black and white with cool modern lines, appealed to her senses as her mother's heavy colonial style of decorating never could. Long legs formed a bridge as her bare feet rested on the glass coffee table. Renoir, an overgrown golden retriever with hair as blond and shaggy as Arly's, sat at her feet with his head resting on her lap; his sympathetic brown eyes gazed up at her green ones.

Covering the mouthpiece of the phone with her hand, Arly leaned down nuzzling Renoir's nose and whispered, "It's my

birthday, for chrissake. You'd think she'd cut me a break today at least, wouldn't you, boy?"

"Look Mother, I really need to get moving.… Because I've
got work to do. I had a great idea this morning for my next
show—the body at work—a series of paintings.… Now
what kind of crack is that? I make a damn good living from
my 'hobby' as you call it. I've been supporting myself with
my art for the past fifteen years.… Just because it's not what
you wanted me to do with my life is no reason to.…

"No, I don't want to fight with you today either, but really,
Mother, you can't expect to keep saying things like that and
get away with it.… All right, all right.… Okay.… I'm sorry
I snapped at you.

"Yes, Mother, I'll be there tonight. Eight o'clock, sharp." Arly
rolled her eyes at Renoir, still sympathetically resting his
head on her lap. "Yes, Mother, I promise. Yeah, I love you
too. Bye."

Arly put the phone down and sighed again. She leaned back
on the couch and closed her eyes attempting to focus on
happier thoughts. She was content with her life. She loved
her work. Living alone with her animals suited her; it didn't
mean she was lonely. Now and then she thought about what
it might be like to share her life with someone—that was
only human. But not every woman needed to be a wife and
a mother to be fulfilled. Why couldn't her mother see that?

The weight of two large paws on her chest and a long wet
tongue licking her face pulled her from her reverie. Arly

laughed and scratched Renoir behind the ears. Feeling much better, she prepared to research her latest project.

With sketch pad in hand, she walked down Fifth Avenue. A sea of bodies flooded the street on this beautiful day. A casual observer might not notice the individual, might let the thousands of faces blend together in a blur, but not Arly. She absorbed the details around her, waiting until the time was right for each one to be pulled out of mental storage and used to its maximum benefit.

Not far from the 61st Street entrance to Central Park, she stumbled upon some construction workers breaking up the street. She situated herself on a graffiti-covered bench and started the preliminary sketches.

Broad shouldered men with bulging biceps gripped vibrating jackhammers. Arly took note of the yellow hard hats and cigarette-butt shaped earplugs that blocked out the din of the construction site. Safety goggles obstructed her view of the men's faces except for jaws clenched tight in concentration. Strong hands, held at arm's length, kept an almost delicate grip on the heavy machinery. Dirty, sweat-soaked tee-shirts clung to wash-board flat stomachs.

All sound was muted as Arly's skilled hands captured each detail and nuance of the men at work. Suddenly, a sharp burst of laughter broke through her concentration. She glanced around slowly, feeling confused and disoriented, as if awakening from a dream.

A few yards away stood a circle of laughing children, their faces alight with smiles. At their center, a mime imitated the men at the construction site, but instead of portraying the serious efforts of the workers, he leaned a pretended fat stomach on the invisible jackhammer before him. His entire body bobbed up, down, and around as if the machine were in control of the man and not the opposite. The harder the imaginary jackhammer pummeled the earth, the looser the mime's body became until he looked like a long wiggling string of spaghetti.

Arly turned away trying to focus again on her subjects. Within moments, the children's laughter surrounded her as the mime brought his act nearer her bench. This wasn't going to work. Arly laid her sketch pad down and walked over to the happy group.

"Excuse me, sir, but I'm trying to work here and your performance, however entertaining it might be to these children, is very distracting. Would you mind taking your show on the road? Why don't you head over to the Hans Christian Anderson statue near the pond?"

The mime, tall with greased back hair that couldn't quite hide his natural curls, bent low at the waist, hands clasped in front of him in supplication as if to say, "A thousand pardons, milady." A grin spread across his whitened face. Assuming that meant he would comply with her request, Arly walked back to the bench and continued her drawing. Another burst of laughter pierced her concentration sending her charcoal skidding across the paper.

The mime had taken up residence on the bench next to hers. Now instead of mimicking the construction workers, he mimicked Arly. Sitting on the bench, he balanced an invisible sketch pad on long legs crossed at the knees. His face was a study in concentration as his hands gripped imaginary charcoal, perfecting various shadings of his sketch. His eyes darted from the men to the pad, his mouth was drawn in a tight line, occasionally broken as he bit down on the tip of his tongue peeking through painted lips.

Realizing he was so serious in this imitation that the children laughed at the mirror image of her he presented rather than the actual motions, Arly gave him a wry grin. She would beat him at his own game; the mime would be her newest "body at work."

After a while, the children began to scatter. As the last little girl left with a wave and an invisible flower, the mime moved over to Arly's bench. Jerking his head toward the bench, his eyes questioning if it would be okay to sit down.

"Might as well," Arly said. She wasn't annoyed at the disruption any longer. After all, she'd gotten more bodies today than she'd expected. As she reached out to shake hands she said, "My name is Arly Jackson. What's yours?"

The mime grinned at her. Instead of accepting her hand-shake, he brought her hand to his lips, kissing it lightly. Then he shrugged and gloved fingers zippered his mouth shut.

"Oh, still can't talk? Not while in uniform, eh?"

The mime nodded again.

"Okay, I can respect that. You know, whatever your name is, you're very good at what you do. I was impressed and to be perfectly honest, mimes don't usually have that effect on me."

A slightly different nod, slower and more gentle spoke his gratitude. He pointed to her sketch pad indicating he wanted to see her drawings. Arly handed him the book, watching him closely as he studied each sketch, starting with the ones she'd made of the construction workers and working his way to the drawings she'd made of him.

One in particular drew his attention. She had drawn the invisible tug-of-war game; he gripped one side of the non-existent rope and three children held the other. Arly had captured the strained expression on his face as deftly as any camera.

The mime's hand flew to his chest as if to still his heart. His mouth fell open in a silent "ah." His blue eyes softened, shining through the white make-up with an almost misty quality.

Arly took the sketchbook and carefully ripped out the drawing.

"Here. Since you like it so much, it's yours. I'll even sign it for you." She quickly autographed the bottom and handed it to him. "That might even be worth a few bucks someday." She laughed heartily at herself and got up to leave. It was getting late. Dinner with her mother loomed ahead of her. She waved goodbye to the mime and headed out to the street.

Five to eight. Arly stood outside the door to her parents' apartment checking herself one last time before ringing the bell. She adjusted the collar of her blue silk blouse then tugged one last time at the hem of the black leather miniskirt she wore in defiance of her mother's wishes. She never likes what I'm wearing anyway, Arly thought. I might as well wear what I like. At least one of us will be happy tonight. Prepared for battle, she reached out and rang the doorbell.

"Just a minute, dear!"

Arly shifted impatiently in the brightly lit hallway. What the hell was taking them so long? Finally, her parents stood side by side in the open doorway.

"Happy birthday, Sweetheart." Her father squeezed her tightly. "How'd your day go? Your mother said you were spending it locked up in your studio."

She returned the hug and added a kiss on his cheek. "No, I wasn't 'locked up' in the studio." She frowned at her mother. "I was at the park making some preliminary sketches. All in all, it turned out to be a very productive day."

Arly leaned forward to accept her mother's kiss and birthday wish. "Are you going to let me in or are we going to eat dinner out here in the hallway?"

Her parents laughed and moved back, pulling her inside the apartment with them.

"SURPRISE!"

Arly was surrounded by a room full of people she hardly knew screaming birthday wishes. She could scarcely breathe as various friends of her parents closed in around her.

"You're really surprised, aren't you, Arlene? Why look at her Louise, she's speechless," said her Aunt Cecilia in a voice even louder than the lime green dress she wore.

Arly stared at her mother, who was so happy her surprise party was a success, she was oblivious to the fact that her daughter wanted absolutely no part of it.

"Thank you, Mother," she said through clenched teeth, "but really, you shouldn't have."

"Oh dear, it wasn't any trouble. After all, how often does my baby turn forty?" With that, Louise Jackson turned her attention to her guests, leaving her daughter to fend for herself.

Arly waded through the crowded room to the bar where she poured herself a scotch. Hell, better make it a double if I'm gonna get through this night, she thought, as she filled the glass to the top. Smiling and nodding at the sea of elderly strangers, she slowly made her way toward the kitchen. When she reached the doorway, Arly glanced furtively over the room like a thief checking that the coast was clear, then escaped into the kitchen to revel in the solitude.

With the door closed behind her, Arly leaned back against the white counter, closed her eyes, and took a swallow of her drink. She savored the liquor as it slid past her lips and down her throat. She sighed deeply, as her body finally relaxed.

"AH-CHOO!"

Arly jumped, nearly spilling her drink. Her eyes flew open to see a tall, thin man stepping out of her mother's pantry. He was nicely dressed, perhaps more casually than the rest of the guests had been. A stray lock of curly black hair flopped over his forehead into clear blue eyes. He looked about the same age as Arly, perhaps a little younger. A line of crimson crept up his face. Embarrassed, he stammered out an apology.

"Sorry if I startled you. I was trying to find a glass. Needed to take an allergy pill." He blushed even more deeply as he held up a little brown prescription bottle.

What a wonderful voice, Arly thought, as the sound of his rich baritone washed over her.

"I'll get one for you." She went to the cabinet, took down a glass, then filled it with tap water. She handed it to him, smiling as she said, "I'm Arly. Who are you?"

The tall stranger took his pill. Arly watched his Adam's apple bob as he swallowed.

"Oh. Sorry. I'm Paul. Paul Watson."

"Hi Paul. Is there any special reason why you'd be invited to my birthday party?" Arly asked, still smiling warmly at the attractive stranger. "I mean, there doesn't have to be one. Lord knows I don't know most of the people out there."

Paul shrugged. "Beats me. I'm a software consultant for your father." After a long pause he said, "We met once when you stopped in at the office. You were upset that day so you probably wouldn't remember."

Arly frowned for a moment, biting the inside of her cheek as she tried to recall the meeting. She took another sip of her scotch; her eyes narrowed as she stared at Paul. Suddenly her face relaxed.

"Yes! I remember now. You were at the computer the day I came in ranting about my mother's latest plot to find me a husband!" Her eyes opened wide as the connection suddenly made sense to her. "Oh no! Don't tell me that's what this is all about! If she's trying to play matchmaker again, I'll…."

Paul stiffened. "No, I don't think that's it. I mean, your father asked me to come over tonight to pick up some new software specs."

Arly studied him for a moment. He fumbled with the empty water glass. This shy fellow was not the type her mother usually tried to fix her up with. Arly relaxed and took another sip of her drink.

"I was about to leave, but your mother wouldn't let anyone near the door until you arrived. She didn't want anything to spoil the surprise." Paul finally put the glass down. Shoving his hands in his pockets, he looked at the floor not knowing what to say next.

"Well, I guess you're okay then." She smiled and moved toward the table. "Why don't we sit down and get to know each other? They certainly won't miss us out there." Paul pulled out a chair for her, accidentally banging her knee in the process.

"Oh God, I'm sorry. I'm such a klutz sometimes…."

"It's okay. Don't worry about it."

They sat in awkward silence until Arly, gregarious by nature, decided enough was enough. "Let's see. I know you're a software consultant…. I'm an artist. Mostly oil paintings but I do some sculpture too."

"I know. You're very good."

"Oh? Have you been to one of my shows?"

Paul squirmed in his chair. "Er, no. Can't say that I have."

"Then my father has been bragging about me again?" Arly tried to sound light and casual, but her curiosity was getting the best of her.

"No."

Conversation definitely wasn't Paul's strong suit. His short answers were driving her crazy. "Well, how can you say I'm good if you haven't seen any of my work?"

"I have. Seen your work, I mean."

Paul reached for his briefcase on the floor beside his chair. The click of the latches rang loudly in Arly's ears as he opened the case and handed her a large white sheet of paper. Her mouth fell open as she recognized the sketch she had done earlier in the day.

"Where did you get this?"

"You gave it to me," he said.

"You? You're the mime from the park this afternoon?"

Paul nodded sheepishly. His eyebrows raised as his eyes widened with feigned innocence. He smiled like Stan Laurel waiting for Hardy to hit him.

At a momentary loss for words, Arly gulped her scotch. She looked at her sketch then stared hard into Paul's face. He sat quietly waiting for her next move.

"You look so different without the makeup. And your hair, it wasn't so curly before."

"That's the idea. To be a different person. The software stuff is what pays the bills, but the mime gig is what I really love." He shrugged and it seemed to Arly there was an interminable pause before he spoke again. "Unfortunately, mimes aren't very popular with a lot of people so I keep it quiet. It wouldn't be good for business if my employers knew."

"So nobody knows about this?"

Paul shook his head. "Nope, just my mother and she made me promise not to tell to anyone else."

"So how come you told me?"

Paul hesitated, then reached for the sketch, gently pulling if from Arly's hands. Once again his eyes shined as he studied the drawing. Without looking up he whispered, "I thought you'd understand."

A wave of melancholy washed over her. Without really knowing why, Arly reached across the table and laid her hand on top of his. "Yes, I understand being passionate about something that others don't take seriously. All too well, in fact."

"Here you are!" Her mother shattered the quiet of the kitchen. "Arly, you've got to open your gifts. Everyone's waiting."

Without giving her daughter a chance to object, Louise Jackson grabbed Arly's arm and shuttled her back into the crowd of well-wishers. Paul followed them, but later as Arly searched the room for a glimpse of him, he was nowhere to be found.

The next day Arly woke to a rainbow dancing across her ceiling as the sun's light reflected through the crystal figurines lining the shelf above her bed. The warm sunshine oozed over her naked flesh like honey, making the music of the city cling to every pore, absorbing the sounds of church bells and traffic that floated through her open window on a faint breeze that gently brushed the curtains aside.

Suddenly, the cats were tap dancing on her stomach, demanding she get out of bed and feed them. Renoir wiggled his shaggy head beneath Arly's hand to convince her he needed some attention too. She scratched his head lovingly and rose from her bed.

"Okay, guys. You win. I'm up."

Showered and dressed for a walk in the park, Arly attached Renoir's leash to his collar and off they went.

Central Park was alive with activity on such a gorgeous day. Hundreds of miniature sailboats floated across the boat pond. A veritable armada, Arly thought. Joggers smiled as they passed. Families were taking advantage of the tree-lined bicycle paths.

A hansom carriage trotted past. A couple snuggled in the backseat, lost in their own private paradise. With foreheads together, they laughed at some private joke, conspiring in a vacuum the way lovers do. The driver smiled and tipped his hat at Arly as she pulled Renoir out of the horse's path. For an instant, irrational jealousy washed over her and she wished she had a human companion to spend this magnificent day with. Then, just as quickly as it had come, the feeling was gone. She and Renoir continued strolling through the park.

She stopped to watch the children climbing on the bronze statue of Alice in Wonderland. A little boy was trying to sit on the Mad Hatter's top hat; his mother warned him to be careful or he'd break an arm. Arly kept walking until she found herself in front of Hans Christian Anderson, her favorite statue in all of Central Park. She remembered climbing on it as a child and reading the story of The Ugly Duckling from the bronze book on his lap.

Arly stared at the statue pondering the strange way time had of changing the way we see things. The statue was the same as it always was, yet her perception had changed. The bronze book didn't look nearly as big as when she was a child. It had shrunk over the years just as the Christmas tree in Rockefeller Center had gone from "the biggest tree in the whole wide world" to merely a big tree. As an artist, she brought the realities of life to her work, exacting in every detail. People paid for the strength and emotion she put into her paintings. But somehow, somewhere, she had lost her sense of wonder at the world. When did I lose my innocence, she thought. When did I become so cynical?

A gentle tap on her shoulder pulled her from her musings. She spun around to find Paul Watson standing beside her in full mime costume. She recognized him immediately and was surprised by the sudden feeling of happiness flooding her senses. A broad smile spread across his face. He bowed deeply, sniffing an invisible flower, which he then handed her with a flourish. Arly couldn't help but notice how different he was, how at ease, when he let his movements speak for him. He was so fluent in body language, he never stumbled over the words there.

"Thank you," she said, sniffing the pretend flower. "It's beautiful."

Paul cocked his head to one side, grinning like a schoolboy. He leaned down to pet Renoir who sat quietly at Arly's feet, wagging his tail happily at the attention.

"Fine protector you turned out to be," Arly said, jokingly. The dog let out a tiny woof but kept wagging his tail just the same. Paul's expression was a mixture of mock indignation and anguish as if Arly's remark had cut him to the quick. She laughed and poked him in the shoulder. "Don't look so serious. I was only kidding."

Her light push sent his body spinning like a cartoon whirlwind. He fell into a backward roll and with one fluid motion bounced back to his feet. Arly laughed, applauding the show with the small crowd gathering around them. Paul hooked his arm through Arly's and walked her to an invisible door. With great panache he opened it, urging Arly to walk through. Just as she passed through the portal, a little boy ran up behind her and slammed the door in Paul's face leaving him trapped inside an invisible box.

Paul's hands felt along the walls searching up and down for an escape route. Finding none, his fists pounded against the door as his lips moved in silent pleas for help. The little boy who slammed the door was laughing hysterically, gripping his sides in his frenzy, but like the mime, he made no sound. Arly felt like she was watching a silent movie—all she needed to make the image complete was the tinkling of piano keys.

Sudden inspiration struck her. She opened her purse and began rummaging through it. With a triumphant look on her face, she pulled her hand out of the purse waving an invisible key ring above her head. She moved to the door and tried a key. The knob wouldn't turn. Paul rattled the doorknob from the other side as if he couldn't see what she was doing. Arly quickly tried another invisible key, then another, and another. Finally, She reached the last key on the ring. She looked at the little boy who had started it all, clasped her hands together in a silent prayer, then tried the lock one last time.

The tumbler silently clicked and Arly pulled the door open. At the unexpected opening, Paul stumbled out of the box and fell into Arly's arms, the two of them landing in a heap on the ground. Arly started laughing as the spectators applauded. Paul helped her off the ground and, holding hands, they took their bows. As the crowd dispersed the two of them strolled arm-in-arm through the park, sharing a comfortable silence as Renoir trailed behind them.

# The Prodigal Returns

The hot Georgia sun sat low in the sky. Forgetting he'd quit smoking, Neil fumbled in his shirt pocket for a cigarette. When he realized what he was doing, he switched to fidgeting with the air conditioner. He leaned over the steering wheel of the Mercedes, grinding his teeth as he watched the road ahead.

"Darlin', you're as nervous as a long-tailed cat in a room full of rocking chairs." Lucy Sherman laughed and poked her husband in the ribs as they drove the final miles toward Rosehaven. The further south of the Mason-Dixon line they'd come, the more her native drawl exerted itself. "What's the matter, Sugar? The last Yankee named Sherman that passed this way escaped unscathed, didn't he?"

"Yes, but he had an army to back him up."

"True, but you've got me to protect you." Lucy leaned across the shift console and planted a kiss on his cheek.

"Well, I still say your parents would be happier about our marriage if we hadn't told them after the fact."

"That's because you don't know my parents. They are stereo-typical southrons. By the time they finally gave up trying to convince me I should come home and find a nice southern boy, they would've insisted on a big wedding with all the trimmings."

"So instead they're going to hate me for stealing away their baby girl." Neil sighed.

"Maybe at first, but they'll be polite about it. Give them time. They'll love you as much as I do."

"Any advice to speed the process?" he asked hopefully.

"Don't say 'y'all' and or 'up north we do it like this.'"

The car stopped short as it turned onto the quarter mile of driveway that led up the hill. Neil whistled through his teeth. Rosehaven, with its white pillared front porch and manicured lawn, could have been a picture postcard.

"My God, Lucy, when you said plantation house, I didn't think you meant Tara!"

Her laughter filled the car. "No, Sugar. Tara's down the road a piece. Now, are we going up to the house or do you plan to sit here all evening?"

By the time they reached the veranda, Theodora McCall Wyndham stood at the open front door. She was an older, meatier version of Lucy with the same light brown hair and green eyes. She swept Lucy into her arms, hugging her tightly and kissing each cheek. Finally, she stepped back and holding Lucy at arm's length, began chastising her.

"Y'all are late. We've been holding off supper till you got here and you know how your daddy gets when his supper's late.

Yancie's fixed all your favorites dishes—cornbread, collard greens, and catfish...."

Theodora, suddenly realizing her lapse in manners, turned to her new son-in-law with a sugary smile. "You must be Neil. Welcome to Rosehaven. Please forgive my rudeness. It's just been so long since Lucy's been home."

"Thank you, Mrs. Wyndham. It's a pleasure to finally meet you. Lucy's told me so much about you."

Theodora reached out to shake Neil's hand, but instead of shaking it, he drew it to his lips and pressed a light kiss on it. Theodora raised one eyebrow and blushed like a school girl.

"Please, call me Dora. All my friends do." Then standing between the couple, she looped her arms in theirs and ushered them inside. She leaned over and whispered in her daughter's ear. "It appears there are gentlemen Yankees too."

Dinner started out rocky. Simon Wyndham barely contained his annoyance at the rampant injustice in his world. First, his baby girl eloped—with a damned Yankee, at that! Now his schedule was upset by their tardiness. During the first course, Theodora alternated between playing hostess, peacemaker, and referee. She implored her husband to remember the meaning of Southern hospitality, and be happy that Lucy and Neil had decided to marry instead of living in sin.

Things quieted after that; the elders concentrated on eating and never noticed the meaningful looks the newlyweds exchanged. Neil raved over each course, and by the time he finished a second helping of banana pudding, an armistice had been called. Simon remarked if his daughter had to marry a

Yankee lawyer, at least she had the good sense to marry one who put the damned criminals behind bars instead of setting them loose on the streets.

After dinner, the family withdrew to the sitting room. Simon, more sociable now that his belly was full, poured brandy. Lucy and Dora sat together on the sofa. Neil stood near the empty fireplace admiring an antique clock on the mantle.

"You have a lovely home. I feel like I've stepped back in time. My mother would go wild over the antiques here," Neil said.

"If you had given us some notice, we could've had the wedding in the gazebo in the rose garden. It's quite lovely in June. Dora and I would've been happy to have your family stay with us." In spite of the pleasant tone of voice, Simon's jibe didn't pass unnoticed. He sipped his brandy and fixed Lucy with a look.

"Now, Daddy, I told you...."

"Most of the antiques are family heirlooms," Dora interrupted, returning the subject to safer ground. "Unfortunately, many treasures were lost during the War, either destroyed or looted when Sherman's army passed through. I daresay, if the general hadn't decided to use Rosehaven as his temporary headquarters, we wouldn't be sitting here today. Did Lucy mention that this house has belonged to the McCall women for over 150 years? In fact, Lucy was named after the first mistress of Rosehaven, her great-grandmother, Lucinda."

"She did say the house had been in the family for a long time."

"Someday, the house and everything in it, will belong to Lucy. And then to Lucy's daughter."

Neil grinned. "What if there are only sons?"

"Fortunately, there's always been a daughter to pass it on to. That's always been the way of it."

Lucy stood up, covering an exaggerated yawn. "It's been a long day. I think it's bedtime." She planted a goodnight kiss on her father's cheek, and then on her mother's.

"I had Yancie put your things in Grandma Varnie's room," Dora said. "I thought y'all would be more comfortable in there."

"Thank you, Mama. We'll see you in the morning."

Lucy took Neil's hand and led him up the curved staircase to the bedroom. Stepping into Grandma Varnie's room, she flipped on the light switch. Painted globe lamps on the dresser glowed with dim light. Neil closed the door behind them and surveyed the room. It was large with high ceilings; a delicate flower print papered the walls. An antique vanity table stood in the corner. Except for a silver comb and brush set and two empty perfume bottles, its surface was bare. A ladder-back rocking chair took up another corner. A full length mirror with intricate rose patterns carved into its frame stood between the vanity and chair. The chair and the mirror were of the same dark wood.

Neil plopped down on the huge four poster bed with its canopied top and stretched his hands over the quilt. "All this has been passed down since before the Civil War? It's amazing.

What a great place to grow up. It's like a living piece of history."

Lucy shrugged and began to undress. "I remember Grandma Varnie. She was very old—born in the 1870s, I think. She was like a raisin, small and wrinkled, but she was always sweet to me. I used play here while she sat in that rocker, doing her needlework and telling stories."

"You must've been very young. Do you remember any of them?"

"She used to talk about a silver tea set that was buried on the grounds so the Yankees wouldn't get hold of it. We'd have pretend tea parties and she'd say, 'Too bad they never found Mama's silver. We could have us a high tea'."

Lucy stood before the mirror, running a fingernail along the engraving. Memories swirled in her head. "She said my great-grandfather carved this for Lucinda as a wedding gift." Lucy wrapped a silk robe around her and stared at the reflection in the mirror. Neil got up from the bed and snuggled behind her, kissing her cheek and neck. Lucy didn't move; she peered into the mirror as if she was looking through it.

"Lucy?" Neil turned her away from the mirror and into his arms. "You okay?"

"I'm fine, but I just remembered the strangest thing. Grandma Varnie used to see things in that mirror—things not really in the room. People from the past."

"Sounds like your grandma was pretty senile by that time."

"I guess." Lucy sighed. "Mama used to tell me it was fine to pretend, but she got real angry when I said I saw the same things in the mirror that Grandma did. It wasn't long after that Grandma Varnie went to the hospital. I never saw her again."

"I imagine that vivid imagination is what led you to a career in advertising." He raised one eyebrow suggestively. "Since we're staying at Tara, let's pretend I'm Rhett and you're Scarlett." With that, he swept her off her feet and carried her to the bed.

Lucy woke in the wee hours of the morning. She sat up against the wooden headboard with a pillow propped behind her. Pale moonlight spilled through the lace curtains, casting shadows across the room. Now that the weight of meeting her parents was off his shoulders, Neil slept peacefully, without the nervous thrashing of the past few nights.

Movement from across the room caught her attention. Probably just the silhouette of the trees dancing in moonlight, she thought. She peered through the dim light; there it was again—like someone scuttling across the room. But that was ridiculous. No one would be in their room this time of night.

Lucy rubbed her knuckles against her eyes. She couldn't believe what she saw.

A woman beckoned from the mirror. Lucy slipped from the bed and moved stealthily toward the apparition until she stood face-to-face with a reflection that was not her own. The black woman in the mirror was hardly more than a girl, with eyes open so wide, white showed all around the dark irises. A faded bandanna hid her hair. Her long dark skirt sported several large patches; her linen blouse was thread-bare. She held a finger to her lips begging silence, but Lucy ignored the signal.

"Who are you?" she whispered.

"Hush!" the girl hissed. "There's Yankees in the house." The girl looked over her shoulder, then motioned to Neil. "One even in yo' bed."

"Who are you?" Lucy asked again. "What do you want?"

"What's wrong wit you, Miz Lucy? You don't know Matty?" A frown crossed the girl's face. "Amos say he done what you told him. Everything gonna be alright. Damn Yankees won't be gettin' yo' treasure."

A loud and sudden snore startled both women. Matty jumped as Lucy spun around to find Neil sprawled on his back in the middle of the bed. When she turned to face the mirror again, only her own dazed reflection stared back.

"It was the strangest thing," Lucy said to her mother, as she sipped her morning coffee. "Neil said it was probably a dream brought on by the rich food and our conversation before bed. I don't know. It was just so…real."

"I'm sure Neil's right," Dora said.

"I suppose." Lucy played with the grits on her plate, swirling her spoon around and around. "Mama? Do you remember how Grandma Varnie used to see people in the mirror?"

"Don't tell me you think you really saw something last night. Grandma Varnie's mind was gone. She was harmless, but she was senile. My word, at one hundred and six, who wouldn't be?" Dora chuckled and changed the subject.

"Wasn't it nice of Daddy to take Neil golfing with him this morning? I think Daddy likes him more than he's willing to admit. He's still hurt because you cheated him out of walking you down the aisle." Yancie came in and started clearing away the breakfast dishes. "I think Neil's very sweet, but I still wish you had let us plan a real wedding." Dora sighed. Suddenly, her face brightened.

"What is it, Mama?"

"I just had the most wonderful idea! We'll hold a reception right here at Rosehaven, invite all our friends and family...."

"Mama, we can't stay long enough for that. Neil has to be in court on Tuesday morning."

"So we'll go through your date book and pick a suitable date. No arguments. Besides, it'll give us all a chance to get to know each other better."

Lucy saw the determined look on Dora's face and realized this was one battle she'd never win. She finished the last of her coffee and prepared to be taken prisoner. "All right, Mama. Let's go check the date book."

Lucy couldn't sleep. The fresh air and exercise had Neil resting in the arms of Morpheus, while she tossed and turned and punched her pillows. She left the bed and sat in the old rocking chair, where she had a clear view of the full moon through the window.

"Why do you look so surprised, Mr. Moon? Are you hallucinating too?" she said softly.

"Miz Lucy!"

Lucy spun toward the mirror. Matty was back. Frantic and shaking, the girl flapped her hands urging Lucy closer.

"Miz Lucy. You got to come. Got to come right now. Amos is hurt bad." The girl was wringing her hands in her skirt. "One of them soldiers come back lookin' for food. Tried to take that ol' sorry hen. When Amos seen him, the Yankee smacked him upside the head with his gun, den run off."

Tears streaked Matty's cheeks; the girl was on the verge of hysteria. "He dyin', Miz Lucy. You got to come."

Lucy touched the cool glass and watched it turn liquid before her eyes. Her hand went through the mirror as if she'd reached into a clear pool. Ripples spiraled outward until the entire mirror was distorted by the waves. Her arm was through the glass to the elbow. A hand grabbed hers from the other side and pulled. The rest of her body followed through the oozing mirror. For a moment she couldn't breathe; it was like giant bean bags molding against each curve of her body, smothering her. Another tug on her arm and Lucy was through the looking glass, gasping for air.

It all happened so fast, she had no time to think. Matty dragged her through the door and down the back stairs to the kitchen. Lucy cried out when she stubbed her toe in the darkness. Matty hushed her, but kept moving.

In the kitchen, a giant black man lay prostrate on the floor near the open fireplace. In the flickering light, the slow rise and fall of his massive chest was barely visible. Blood dripped along the right side of his face, oozing from beneath the dirty rag someone had tied around his head. Matty rushed to kneel beside him.

"Everythin' gonna be alright now, Amos. I brung Miz Lucy."

His eyes fluttered open. Lucy knelt beside him, not knowing what else to do.

"I sorry, Miz Lucy. I can't help you no more."

"Hush now. Save your strength. You just rest, Amos." Overwhelmed by her helplessness, Lucy told herself this was all a bad dream. She wasn't really watching a man bleed to death on the kitchen floor.

Amos raised a hand to motion her closer.

"Micah knows…." His words were a strangled whisper as he fought to make his final words known.

Matty started crying in earnest. "Damn Yankees kilt Amos and left us to die," she wailed.

"Quiet!" Lucy snapped at the hysterical slave. "What does Micah know, Amos?"

"The hidey hole." He shuddered and breathed his last, then his head lolled sideways and his eyes stared blindly into the fire.

For the first time, Lucy noticed the skinny little boy huddled in the corner by the hearth, with his knees drawn up tight against his chest and his head bent forward so only the top of his nappy head was visible. She went to the boy and touched his shoulder.

"Micah, do you know where the hidey hole is?"

The boy cocked his head, half his face glowed in the firelight. Slowly, he nodded.

"Tell me where it is, Micah."

Matty hiccuped between sobs. "You know Micah dumb, Miz Lucy. He can't say nothin' to nobody. That why Amos took him with him."

Lucy turned to the boy. "Micah, can you show me where the hidey hole is?" The boy nodded again. He got to his feet and stepped out the back door into the night, motioning her to follow.

The full moon lay half hidden behind a block of clouds. Thick heat sucked at her like a mosquito. Lucy glanced back at the house, it was the same, yet different. Only the faint flicker of fire light from the kitchen window broke the shroud of darkness. The paved driveway had been transformed into dirt road; the garage became the old barn. Micah tugged at her arm, leading her into the copse of peach trees that lined the ridge behind the barn.

Lucy held the boy's hand in a death grip, afraid she might lose him in the dark. I must be crazy following a six year old boy in the middle of the night, to find God knows what, hidden who knows where, she thought. How the boy could find anything in this dark, she didn't know. She couldn't see her hand in front of her face. *If I didn't know this was a dream, I'd be scared witless.*

Micah stopped short and Lucy nearly fell over him. The clouds moved away letting moonlight spill over them. The boy's mouth split in a wide pearly grin as he pointed to a fallen oak tree, with its limbs gnarled and rotted. He dragged her closer, then began sweeping away dead leaves from under one of the branches. Once the leaves were gone, Micah dug with his fingers, clawing the dirt. His eyes widened as he pointed at the hole. He motioned for Lucy to help him. They worked side-by-side, scooping mounds of loose dirt with bare hands. Sweat dripped into their eyes. Their fingers bled. Just when Lucy thought Micah must have chosen the wrong spot, her fingers touched something hard and flat.

As the faint gold of morning shimmered on the horizon, Lucy looked into the hole she and Micah had dug through the night. At the bottom of the pit rested a large wooden box engraved with roses. She opened the latch and lifted the cover. A shiny silver teapot with matching creamer and sugar bowl sparkled in the morning sunshine.

Lucy gasped. "Do you see that, Micah?" She turned and realized she was alone. She looked in the hole again, her great-grandmother's treasure was still there. Suddenly, the world spiraled around her, her knees buckled, and everything went dark.

They found Lucy unconscious beside a deep hole next to the gazebo in the garden. She was in her nightgown, smeared with dirt and blood. Her outstretched hand pointed limply to the silver tea set resting in a box carved with roses.

# Dark into Light

The bedroom was dark and smelled of unwashed linen. It was a large room with the usual furnishings, but after months of neglect it needed a thorough cleaning. On the bedside nightstand, a dim light illuminated a photograph of a middle-aged couple. The woman had a wild mane of auburn hair and laughing green eyes. She held up a sign that read "Kingsley makes the Bestseller List." The man at her side was tall and thin, his long brown hair was streaked with gray. He had one arm wrapped tightly around her; the other held a hardcover book. The woman smiled at the camera; the man only had eyes for her.

Naked except for a pair of boxer shorts, Roger Kingsley entered the bedroom, having relieved himself in the adjoining bathroom. He sprawled on the pillows of his unmade bed, sipping the cognac that had lately become more than a night cap. He ran a hand through his hair and picked up the letter thrown carelessly on the bed. He read it again for what must be the hundredth time.

...We regret to inform you that search for the remains of passengers of flight 421 has been discontinued...

He crumpled the paper and sent it flying across the room.

"Goddamn it!" Roger shouted at the empty room. "How can they call off the search when they haven't found Tessa? They haven't found her body—she can't be dead."

But in his heart, Roger knew Tessa was gone. After two months of extensive searching, he knew it was futile for them to continue. Whatever hadn't been found must surely have been washed further out to sea or eaten by fish. He grimaced. It was too painful to think of Tessa as fish food.

Why hadn't he gone with her to visit her sister? Because the new book was behind schedule? What did the damn book matter now? He was alone. All the words had left him the afternoon her flight home crashed into the sea.

He poured himself another cognac and downed it in one swallow. Better to drink himself into oblivion than think those thoughts.

Roger woke feeling a warm hand stroking his temple. Instinctively, he grabbed the hand that touched him and opened his eyes. He saw nothing but the iridescent glow of the digital clock on the nightstand.

"Who are you?" he asked in an angry whisper.

Silence. Before he could say another word, lips, warm and moist, pressed against his—a familiar taste filled his mouth as a pointed tongue entwined with his in an erotic dance.

"Tessa? Is that you?" he whispered into the darkness, as his hands traveled along the well-known curve of her back.

"Yes." Her breath whispered, warm and sweet, caressed his ear, and sent a shiver through him. He sighed. A dream, a wonderfully real, booze-induced dream.

"I'm not a dream, Roger. I'm here." Tessa pressed her hand against Roger's chest, her touch making every hair stand on end; goosebumps raised on his flesh.

The booze, his grief, the shock of the letter—that's what's causing this hallucination, Roger thought. It doesn't matter. I want Tessa any way I can have her.

Roger rolled over pinning Tessa beneath him. His need blocked out all reason. He made love to his wife with all the passion and tenderness they had shared through twenty-five years of marriage. She responded to him as she always had, a wild and free spirit, sharing his desire, until finally, he lay next to her, sated and spent. He cradled her in his arms, holding her close to his heart. He was beginning to doze when he felt her voice vibrating against his chest.

"I have to go."

"No." He held her tighter, refusing to let go, willing her to stay.

"I came back for a reason—to tell you I love you and to make sure you don't waste the rest of your life. You have to start writing again. You can't stop because I'm gone. It's your passion."

"You're wrong. You're my passion. There is no life without you. Only existence. Don't leave me again, Tessa. Please...." Roger's voice cracked with tears he held at bay.

"I'll always be with you, Roger. Here…" she lightly tapped his forehead, then the center of his chest. "…and here. Write about me if there's nothing else, but don't wallow in sadness."

Roger opened his mouth to speak, but her finger against his lips silenced him. Pulling him close, Tessa stroked his hair until he fell into a deep sleep.

When the dawn came, a sliver of sunlight pierced the draperies and streaked across the bedroom. Millions of tiny dust motes floated in the shaft of light, which like an arrow, pointed to Roger's laptop that had sat idle in the corner for the past two months. In the center of the black plastic cover, shimmering in the sunlight, rested Tessa's wedding band.

# Scars

Alone in the small office she shared with three other programmers, Diane closed the newspaper she was reading as she ate her lunch. A young girl murdered, caught in the crossfire of a gang war. A man mugged on the subway for the three dollars in his wallet. An old woman brutally raped in her own home. Her head throbbed.

Rummaging through her desk, she found the bottle of aspirin she kept there. She took two with a mouthful of coffee from her thermos, and leaned back in her chair. Focusing on the photo montage she kept on her computer, she let the pictures of her son filter out the violent images the paper had dredged up. There was Matt on his first birthday, his chubby face covered with cake. Matt getting on the school bus for the first time. Matt in second grade, proudly showing off that he was missing front teeth. Matt with his Little League trophy. Diane grinned and made a mental note to add more recent photos to the montage. The phone rang, jarring her back to reality.

"Diane Thorton, microprocessor lab, may I help you?"

"Mrs. Thorton, this is John Carver, principal at Twin Pines Elementary school. I'm sorry to disturb you at work, but your son, Matthew, has just been involved in a serious fight during recess."

"Is he all right?"

"Matt's fine. It's the other boy, Thomas Bishop, who got the worst of it. It looks like he might need a few stitches."

"Mr. Carver, I don't understand. What happened?"

"Well, that's part of the problem, Mrs. Thorton. I don't really know. Neither boy is talking. To be honest, Thomas is a bully. This isn't his first fight. I think he's embarrassed that a nice kid like Matt got the best of him. My guess is, Thomas somehow instigated the fight expecting Matt to be an easy target and got more than he bargained for."

"What happens now?"

"It's school policy to suspend students in cases like this. Would it be possible for you to come down to my office so we can discuss this further?"

Diane glanced at her watch. If she hurried, she could catch the 1:30 bus.

"I'm on my way, Mr. Carver. I should be there in about forty-five minutes." She left a hastily scribbled note on her boss's desk, grabbed her purse, then ran to catch the bus.

Thank heavens the bus is on time, Diane thought, as she climbed the steps and dropped the exact change into the slot. The bus was fairly empty, with only a few senior citizens and a young mother trying to keep her three children in their seats. Diane sat by a window. She glanced at her reflection in the glass, smoothing back the wispy blond curls that had escaped her braid. Her thoughts swirled like a cyclone—Matt involved in a fight. Sweet, gentle Matt causing another boy to need stitches. What could have happened to make him react so viciously?

One of the children started to cry when her mother roughly pushed her back on the seat. "You stop crying this instant, Missy, or I'll give you something to cry about," the woman said. The little girl continued crying. Diane heard a loud THWACK and winced. The child screamed louder, tears streaming down her face. Angry at the violent attack, Diane bit the inside of her cheek and kept silent. Her stop was a block away and she was too worried about Matt to argue with a stranger.

At the school, Diane approached the front desk. "May I help you?" the receptionist asked, without looking up from her paperwork.

"I'm here to see Principal Carver," Diane said.

The woman started to glance up, then quickly looked away, the welcome smile falling away before it could fully form.

The scar, Diane thought and sighed inwardly. It was always the same. The jagged line that ran down the side of her otherwise pretty face never went unnoticed by strangers. Some were more polite than others, but their reactions were the same: shock, disgust, curiosity, or pity.

She smiled at the receptionist, who made her sign in and directed her to the principal's office.

Principal Carver sat behind a wooden desk that overpowered the small office. The walls behind him were lined with books, mostly on education and psychology, but Diane noticed a few classics and bestsellers too. In front of the desk were two chairs covered with olive green vinyl. Her son sat dejectedly on one of them. Even the rude noise that escaped as he shifted in his seat didn't bring a hint of the smile it would have in other situations.

Diane strode across the room and extended her hand to the principal, who rose to greet her. "I'm Diane Thorton. Matthew's mother."

"Mrs. Thorton. I'm glad you could make it." Carver stared at her face, forgetting to let go of her hand now that the formalities were over.

The scar again.

"It's 'Ms.' I'm divorced," Diane said, freeing her hand from Carver's and taking the seat next to Matt. She turned to her son, looking him over to make sure he wasn't hurt. She reached out, running her hand through his dark hair and around his face until she grabbed his chin. "Are you all right?"

Matt nodded, but turned to avoid his mother's gaze.

The principal cleared his throat. "Ms. Thorton, the situation hasn't changed since we spoke on the phone. Matt still refuses to say what caused the fight. I'm afraid I'm going to have to order a three day suspension starting tomorrow."

"Mr. Carver, may we speak privately?"

"Certainly. Matt, wait outside, will you?" Matt left the room, a condemned man with his eyes glued to the floor.

Diane sat tall in the chair, back straight, knees together, her hands resting on the purse in her lap. She took a deep breath.

"I'll get straight to the point. This is very unlike Matt. He knows how I feel about violence." Diane caught herself fingering the scar on her cheek, and put her hand in her lap. "He must have had a damn good reason for fighting. There must be extenuating circumstances. Is there anything we can do to avoid this suspension? I don't want to ruin his good record, and to be honest, I can't afford to lose three day's pay to stay home with him."

The principal drummed his pencil on the desk, avoiding her gaze as he considered the problem. Finally, he looked Diane in the eye. "I'll tell you what I'll do. If you can get Matt to tell you what really happened and apologize to Thomas by tomorrow, I'll make a one time exception and cancel the suspension."

Diane smiled. She knew Matt. She'd find out what happened. Everything would be okay. She rose from her chair and shook the principal's hand.

"Thank you, Mr. Carver. Matt and I will see you first thing tomorrow morning."

Diane and Matthew walked to the bus stop in silence. Matthew kept his head down, his hands shoved in his pockets. Diane watched the grim expression on her son's face and wondered for the hundredth time what could have possibly driven him to beat the boy so viciously. They arrived at the bus stop; it was deserted except for the two of them.

"You sure you're all right, Matt?"

"I'm okay, Mom," Matt answered flatly, still not looking at her.

"Do you want to tell me what happened? Why did you beat that boy?" Diane struggled to keep her voice calm. Matt just shrugged. Diane frowned at the top of her son's head and she sighed. All right, Matt. I know where you get that stubborn streak from, and I can be patient.

Within the hour, mother and son were home in their apartment. Matthew went straight to his bedroom. Diane decided to give him some time alone to think. She needed some time herself. She sat on the beat up sofa in their tiny living room, sifting through the mail. Most of it was junk. At the bottom of the stack was a birthday card for Matt from his father—three weeks late. For a moment, Diane thought about destroying it before Matt saw it and had his feelings hurt all over again. Finally, she just laid it on the coffee table and went to start dinner.

"Mom?" Matt's voice was sheepish as he stuck his head through the kitchen doorway. "Do you need any help?"

Diane smiled as she bent to put the pan of leftover lasagna into the oven. She knew her son would come around sooner or later. She straightened and turned to face him.

"Sure. We can make the salad together."

Matt took the head of lettuce and began ripping leaves into the salad bowls while Diane sliced tomatoes, radishes and finally, a cucumber. She popped a piece of the cucumber into her mouth and handed Matt a slice which he gobbled up eagerly.

"Hungry, eh? Guess fighting would work up an appetite."

Matt frowned. "I'm sorry, Mom. I know how you feel about fighting."

"Are you ready to tell me what happened?" Diane said quietly. Matt stole another slice of cucumber and popped it into his mouth. He chewed very slowly in order to avoid answering. "Matt, I'm not going to lecture you. You know fighting is wrong. Lashing out at other people never solves anything and usually makes matters worse. But I really want to know why you did what you did."

The oven timer beeped and Diane placed the reheated lasagna on the table. Matt brought over their salad bowls and poured each of them a glass of iced tea. Mother and son ate in silence. The ticking of the wall clock echoed in the quiet. Finally, Matt put his fork aside and spoke.

"I hit him because he kept saying mean things about you. He said you were uglier than a monkey's butt. He called you 'Scar-face.'"

"Matt…you know all about 'sticks and stones—'"

"You're wrong, Mom. Words do hurt—worse than any punch from Thomas Bishop. He had no right to say those things about you. You're beautiful. You're good. He's the one who's ugly. I hope he winds up with a scar on his face."

"Matthew David Thorton, I don't want to ever hear you say something like that again."

Her emotions were jumbled and Diane took a few deep breaths to calm herself before she continued.

"Matt," she said, more softly now. "You were just a little boy when I left your father but I know you remember what it was like." Diane smoothed loose strands of hair out of her face; unconsciously she fingered her scarred cheek. "He was always striking out. He'd say he was sorry, then he'd do it again. What did it prove? He was bigger and stronger so he could get away with it."

Diane paused, watching Matt's face as the memories of his father's abuse washed over him. She hated reminding him of the past. It was bad enough living through it the first time. Matt stared into his empty dinner plate.

"Matt, look at me." Diane reached over the table and gently lifted her son's chin until their eyes met. "But your father wasn't bigger and stronger, not really. I was. It took much more strength to take you and leave, than to stay and be beaten. My love for you gave me that strength, Matt. Do you understand what I'm trying to say?"

"I guess so." Matt's voice was low and quiet.

He looked so very small, Diane's heart ached. She squeezed his chin and smiled. "How about some ice cream for dessert? There's mint chocolate chip, your favorite." Matt grinned, then began clearing off the table while Diane scooped their ice cream.

"Mom, can I ask you something?" Matt said later, as the pair stood side by side washing the supper dishes.

"Ask away, Sweetie."

"How come you don't have plastic surgery to get rid of that scar? You'd be beautiful."

"I thought you said I was beautiful already," Diane teased.

"You know what I mean, Mom."

Diane sighed. "Yes, I do." She was quiet for a few minutes, thinking how she could explain her feelings in a way he'd understand. "There are lots of reasons why I don't have it fixed, Matt. For one, I don't really think about it much until someone else reacts to it. I'm content with who I am inside and that's more important than outward appearances. But you know, I think the most important reason is that the scar reminds me I'm strong enough never to let myself be any-one's victim again."

Early the next morning, Matt and Diane waited in the prin-cipal's office for Thomas Bishop to appear. When he finally did show up, Thomas appeared uneasy at coming face to face with the kid who had given him a black eye and three stitches on his chin. His eyes darted toward Diane and he had the good grace to look embarrassed, realizing she must know what he'd said about her.

"Thomas, Matthew has something he wants to say," the principal said.

Matt walked over to Thomas and reached out to shake his hand. "I'm sorry I hit you. I should've just walked away instead. Maybe we can forget about it and be friends."

Thomas stared at Matt in disbelief. He knew Matt would have to apologize but he hadn't expected the offer of friendship. He took Matt's hand in a tentative handshake.

"It's okay," he said. "I guess I had it coming anyway. I would've done the same thing if someone said that stuff about my mother." He looked toward Diane, who stood smiling at her son. "I guess I owe you an apology too," he said, not quite looking in Diane's face.

"Apology accepted," Diane said. "Is it all right for the boys to go back to class now?" she asked Principal Carver.

The principal nodded and sent the boys off. Diane thanked him for his handling of the situation, then headed down the same hallway as the boys on her way to work. As she turned the corner, she happened to hear Thomas say, "You know, your mom is pretty cool."

Diane felt a burst of pride when she heard Matt reply, "Yeah, I think so too."

# Christmas Present

Daniel was dreaming and he knew it.

He was ice skating in Rockefeller Center with his wife and their angel-faced daughter. The giant Christmas tree lit up behind them, sending its pine fragrance out into the city. A light snow fell as they skated around and around; the three of them holding hands and laughing behind their scarves, eyes twinkling with merriment.

Their laughter was suddenly drowned out by rough voices coming up fast behind them. Three boys whizzed past, recklessly cutting in front of them. His scarf tightened, snapping his head back, as strong hands tugged him from behind. Daniel glimpsed hard young faces speeding by as he fell backwards. He let go of his family's hands, sensing their struggle for balance. Down he went, landing hard on his tailbone. He cried out, hit by another jolt of pain as the back of his head cracked on the ice.

For a dream, Daniel thought, this hurts like hell.

He heard a female voice yelling close by. "I see you Sam Gibbons—and you too, Jack! You get out of here before I

call the police!" Awake now, Daniel opened his eyes to see
a woman bundled in a hooded parka bending over him; her
big green eyes studied him while snowflakes collected on the
wisps of dark wavy hair that outlined her face.

"Are you all right, mister?"

Her face showed genuine concern for a fellow human being, something he hadn't seen in a long time. Daniel looked
around and remembered where he was. Earlier in the evening, he'd sat down in the covered porch behind the old
diner, seeking shelter from the biting wind. He must have
fallen asleep. The snow had encrusted itself onto his beard
and over his woolen gloves. He shivered.

"I'm not sure. I feel like I've been hit by a truck."

"Not a truck, just those darn Gibbons boys. A pack of trou-
blemakers if ever there was one. I came to put out the trash
and saw they were kicking at something. Scared 'em off when
I realized it was a somebody. Let's get you up and inside so
you don't freeze to death."

Daniel suppressed a groan as the woman helped him into
the brightly lit diner. He slumped into one of the cheery red
vinyl booths and looked around, letting the warmth spread
over him. Christmas had exploded inside the diner; every
corner was decorated. Silver garland with colored lights
draped across the ceiling. Pictures of Santa Claus, reindeer,
and snowmen hung on the neatly painted walls. Miniature
Christmas trees sat on each table, while a larger one dressed
up the corner by the jukebox.

The woman hung her coat on a wall hook, then went behind the counter. She filled two cups with steaming coffee and slid into the booth across from Daniel.

"Drink this. It'll warm you up. My name's Christmas Snow and you're enjoying the hospitality of the Snowy End Diner. Folks just call me Chris. What's your name?"

"Daniel Drummond." Daniel swallowed a mouthful of coffee, holding the cup with both hands, letting the warmth seep in. "Christmas Snow, huh? Now there's a name all right."

"Well, Snow is my married name. The maiden name was even worse." Her eyes twinkled like lights on the tree when she smiled. "My mother named me Christmas because that's when I was born. Our last name was Day. You get used to the teasing when you grow up with a name like that."

Daniel studied her face to see if she was joking and decided she wasn't. He sipped the coffee, then raised the cup to her in a toast. "To my hero! Christmas Day Snow." He couldn't help but chuckle as he said it. Something about this woman made him forget how miserable he really felt. "Doesn't get any better when you put them all together, does it?"

Chris laughed with him. "Nope. But like I said, I'm used to it. You look about wasted away. How about something to eat with that coffee?"

Without waiting for his answer, she got up and went behind the counter again, making small talk as she prepared a plate of meatloaf piled high with mashed potatoes, gravy and bread. She set it down in front of him and waited for him to eat. When he hesitated she asked, "What's the matter? Don't you like meatloaf?"

"It's not that. It's just that I'm a little short of cash."

"Oh, for heaven's sake! It's Christmas Eve. Do you see anybody pounding down the door to eat what's left of my meatloaf? They're all at home with their families and holiday turkeys. It'll just go to waste—eat. Think of it as a Christmas present."

Daniel hesitated, but his stomach growled just then, so he gave in and took a small bite. His eyebrows raised in surprise. "This is delicious," he said, while he chewed. Once the feasting had begun, he couldn't stop. His stomach, on tasting its first home-cooked meal in he couldn't remember how long, was not about to let him quit. He shoveled one forkful after another into his mouth until the plate was empty, then soaked up the last of the gravy with the bread and popped it into his mouth, licking the juice from his fingertips.

When Daniel realized what he done, an embarrassed flush rose to his cheeks. "Pardon my manners, Mrs. Snow. It's just been a while since I've eaten anything this good."

"Oh Pooh! Don't worry about that. It's been a long time since I've seen anyone really enjoy my meatloaf. And please, call me Chris. Mrs. Snow was my mother-in-law, God rest her soul."

"Chris, it is then. And call me Daniel." He looked around at the empty diner and wondered where her husband was—probably picking up a last minute present. He glanced at the clock on the wall. Ten o'clock on Christmas Eve. Awfully late to be shopping, especially in this deserted neck of the woods.

"You're a very brave woman to take in a stranger while you're all alone. Won't your husband be angry with you? I know I would be if I were him."

"Well, Daniel, I guess if he were here, maybe he would be, but a few years back he decided I didn't need him anymore. I've been taking care of myself ever since." She got up to get them some more coffee.

Having finally warmed up, Daniel took off his jacket while he watched Chris bring an entire apple pie back to the table, along with the coffee pot. She sliced it into six large pieces and served them each one. Feeling awkward, he felt he should say something since he'd brought up the subject.

"I didn't mean to be nosy. Divorce can be hard on folks."

"I'm not divorced. I'm a widow." She said it matter-of-factly, but the way she gulped her coffee reminded him of someone needing "liquid courage."

"Robby and I were together since we were kids. High school sweethearts. We got married right after graduation. After 9/11, he enlisted in the Marines. He was in Iraq. A month before he was due to come home, he was wounded. Ended up in a wheelchair unable to feel anything from the chest down. He couldn't deal with it. He kept telling me to leave him, to find myself a real man. I told him he was all the man I needed, but I guess he didn't believe me." Chris paused, staring into the coffee cup. "Three years ago, he left me a note saying he was giving me my freedom for Christmas. Then he overdosed himself with a bottle of sleeping pills."

Daniel pushed back the lump that had formed in his throat. "I'm so sorry, Chris. I can only imagine how terrible that must have been for you."

"Yeah, it was. Still is sometimes. I don't know why I even brought it up." She sighed deeply. "There's something about you that seems to make me run off at the mouth. So tell me about yourself. Why were you sleeping in the alley? You don't look like an ordinary bum to me."

Daniel looked down at his thread-bare flannel shirt, ragged jeans, the work boots, worn from miles of walking and hitch-hiking. He hadn't had a real bath in weeks, cleaning himself as best he could in gas station restrooms. An ordinary bum was exactly what he looked like.

"Now what makes you say that? Your little town doesn't look like it would tolerate too many bums, ordinary or otherwise." He grinned, surprised again at how easily the smile came over him.

"Well, Daniel, I'll tell you. Since Robby left, I spend a lot of time alone, but running this diner, I spend a lot of time dealing with people. I'm a good judge of character and I can usually spot a loser right off. When I do, I go call the sheriff. You are not a loser—just someone who's down on his luck. It's something in your eyes."

Chris took another sip of coffee.

"That accent of yours tells me you're far from home. New York, maybe?"

"Not only a good judge of character, but psychic too. Yeah, I'm a New Yorker. Left there about a year ago. I'm not on the run from the law or anything—in case you were worried." He smiled, pausing for effect. "There just wasn't anything left for me there. I needed a change of scenery."

Daniel took a bite of apple pie. That's one way of ending a discussion, he thought, just keep your mouth full.

"Guess you don't have any family then?" She eyed him closely, as if trying to make up her mind about something.

Daniel shook his head and stuffed another fork-full of pie in his mouth.

"I've got an idea." Chris's eyes sparkled. "It's Christmas Eve, it's snowing like crazy, and you're not going to get a ride any-where tonight. Why don't you stay here? You can take a hot bath and I think some of Robby's old clothes might even fit you. You can wear them at least until I wash the ones you've got on. I've got a sofa-bed in the living room that doesn't get much use so the mattress is still good."

Daniel stared at her in disbelief, his jaw dropping in surprise. This woman was willing to take a stranger she'd met only an hour ago into her home. My God, he could be a murderer or a rapist, for all she knew. He wasn't, of course, but how could she know that? He hadn't known such trusting people still existed. He'd seen too many of the other kind in the past year; it shocked him into speechlessness.

"Well, what's the matter? You're looking at me like I belong in the loony bin. You don't really have a choice anyway. If you think I'm gonna let you tramp out in the snow and freeze to death, you're the one that belongs in the loony bin. And if you do go out there, I'll call the sheriff and see you spend the night in jail. At least I'll know you're warm and dry."

She really wasn't going to give him a choice. Daniel felt a strange comfort in knowing she cared enough to force him to stay. There was no guile to this woman. She may have been alone, but she was not desperate, hunting for a man to share her bed. Those green eyes, wide with innocence, waited for his reply.

"I guess I know when I'm licked. You win, Chris. But first thing tomorrow I'll be on my way. I don't want your Christmas and birthday plans spoiled because of me."

"Good, it's settled then. And don't worry about spoiling my plans—I don't have any. I was just going to curl up with a good book and listen to carols on the radio. I'd much rather have some company. Come on. Let's get you settled."

They got up from the booth, taking the dirty dishes with them to the sink. Chris locked up the diner and motioned Daniel to follow her.

A door in the back led to her apartment. It was a tidy little place, just right for a person alone or a couple on their own. The furniture was old but comfortable looking. Photos hung neatly on the walls. Through the doorway to the left, he could see a small kitchen. The bedroom was on the right; through the open door was a neatly made bed with hand-stitched pillows thrown on a blue chenille bedspread. A leather-bound Bible lay on the nightstand, still opened to the page she'd been reading.

"Well, this is home! The bathroom's right through there on the other side of the kitchen. The stove helps keep the tiles warm." Her smile made the whole place seem warm to Daniel. "You go on and get settled. There are fresh towels in there already. I'll look for those clothes while you're soaking. The water's nice and hot, so it should help ease those achy muscles. Those darn Gibbons boys! A bad lot if ever there was one. You know, you should press charges against them. A few nights in juvenile hall might do them some good." She shook her head and went off as if her most trusted friend was spending the night.

Daniel had almost forgotten the earlier beating but a hot bath sounded like a wonderful indulgence. He went into the bathroom and started running hot water into the tub. The little room filled quickly with steam. Within minutes, he shed his dirty clothes and eased into the tub, sighing with delight at the luxury. He didn't know how long he had sat there, soaking away the aches and fatigue of the road, when he heard Chris tapping on the door.

"Daniel? Are you decent? Better cover up 'cause I'm coming in for a minute." Daniel pulled the shower curtain closed as she opened the door. "I found some pajamas and a robe for you. There's also some jeans and a couple of shirts you can have—they're like new."

She picked his dirty clothes up off the floor and checked the size. I was right, you are the same size Robby was. These should fit you just fine." She turned to leave but just as she was about to close the door behind her she turned back again. "And Daniel?"

"Yes?"

"If you want to shave, there's shaving cream and razors in the medicine cabinet."

He heard the door close behind her. "I wonder if that's a hint?" He grinned to himself and continued with his bath.

When Daniel finally emerged from the bathroom, his blond hair was washed and neatly combed. He was wearing fresh night clothes, and his face was clean shaven. He felt good all over and wonderfully relaxed. When he reached the living room, he saw that Chris had opened the fold-away bed and turned down the covers. He hadn't been treated this well in a long time.

Seeing her door was closed, he took the time to survey the area. He noticed that where the diner had been covered with Christmas, there wasn't a single decoration in the little apartment. Not so strange he thought, considering her husband had killed himself around this time of year. He supposed she felt obligated to decorate the diner for the customers.

He went over to the shelf where pictures sat in neatly dusted frames. There was one that looked like Chris as a little girl with her parents, and another of a ten or twelve year old Chris with a carrot-haired boy he assumed was Robby. In the center of the shelf was a large wedding photo. Robby and Chris looked as happy as most brides and grooms on their wedding day, filled with the promise of tomorrow. Looking closer, he thought he saw a slight resemblance between himself and Robby around the eyes. Maybe that's what she saw that made her treat him so kindly.

Chris opened her door, startling him out of his reverie. "Just wanted to say goodnight." She wore a high-necked night-gown, covered with a plaid flannel bathrobe. Her hair was brushed out and spread over her shoulders. She looked like an angel.

"I see you did decide to shave! You look very handsome, Mr. Drummond," she said a little shyly.

"Thanks. I feel much better now. But how did I get to be 'Mr. Drummond' again? I thought we were becoming friends."

She gave a little laugh and said, "You're right—Daniel. Now get some sleep. And Merry Christmas."

Daniel glanced at the clock on the wall and saw it was past midnight. "Merry Christmas, Chris! And happy birthday too!"

She smiled, then closed the door behind her as she went back into her room. Daniel eased himself into the tightly-made bed, closed his eyes, and let the weariness that had been his companion for the past year overtake him. He fell into a deep sleep.

He was driving down the interstate with his wife and daugh-ter. The three of them were singing to pass the time on their trip home from the mountains. "…If one of those bottles should happen to fall, twenty-nine bottles of beer on the wall." Checking the rear view mirror, Daniel saw a pair of bright lights speeding up behind him, closing in fast. He white-knuckled the wheel in panic as a scream burst from his lips. "MARY!"

Daniel bolted upright in the bed as Chris raced into the room. His face was a mask of terror, sweat dripped from his forehead. His body trembled, still gripped by the nightmare. She went to his side and put her arms around him.

"Shush, Daniel, shush. It's all right. It was just a bad dream." She rocked him like a frightened child, repeating the soothing words over and over.

"Mary? Is that you?"

As soon as the words were out of his mouth, Daniel realized it was not Mary at his side. "I'm so sorry, Chris. I didn't mean to wake you. Just a dream. Really. I'm okay. Go back to sleep."

"Who's Mary?"

"My wife."

"Do you want to talk about it? It helps sometimes." Chris sat back and turned on the light. The look on her face said " you can tell me." She waited for him to begin.

Daniel wrapped himself in the robe and got out of the bed. He paced the floor, running his hands back and forth through his hair. For the first time since the accident, he spoke of his wife and daughter.

"A little over a year ago, my wife, my eight year old daughter, Kelly, and I, were on our way home from a ski trip in the mountains. Some idiot out joy-riding decided to play games on the icy roads. He came speeding up next to me, hit some ice and knocked us off the road. When I came to, Mary was dead in the seat next to me. Kelly had somehow released her

seat belt and crawled out of the car. They found her by following the trail of blood in the snow. Mary and Kelly were
all I had in the world and they were taken from me in an
instant."

Chris walked over to Daniel and looked up into his eyes.
Tears spilled down his cheeks and she gently brushed them
aside. Daniel reached out and she held him close. They just
stood there, holding each other, offering comfort from an
unjust world. When Chris finally stepped back, her own face
was wet with tears left too long unshed.

"Come on, Daniel. It's Christmas. A time of rebirth and new
beginnings." She wiped her face with the sleeve of her robe.
She pulled herself together and smiled at him. "Let's give
ourselves a Christmas present. Why don't you and I decide
to let go of the sadness of the past and get on with our lives,
the way our loved ones would have wanted?"

He looked at this woman who had opened her home and
her heart to a stranger. He had run away from the past and
she had locked herself up in a small town diner. She had
suffered as much as he had, yet the face that looked up at
him beamed with hope. Maybe it was time to stop blaming
himself for being alive. Time to go on living.

"I think you're right, Chris. But we have to do this properly.
Have you got anything that's suitable for a toast?"

She went into the kitchen and brought back a couple of bottles of beer.

"Will these do?"

"They'll do just fine," Daniel said, as he took one of the bottles from her. "A toast to finding hope and friendship. And to making new memories instead of living through old ones!"

"And to Christmas presents from the heart!"

They drank to their promise and wished each other a Merry Christmas with their eyes.

# Where Conscience Leads

Germany, 1935

Night had fallen by the time Heinz Scheide and Erich Strauss left the movie theater. It was late March and winter lingered in the air like a house guest who had over-stayed his welcome, but the teenagers were still so engrossed in the movie they hardly noticed the chill in the air as they walked home.

"I love American movies," Heinz said, smiling broadly.

"Me too," said Erich, pulling his cap down over his blond hair. "And American westerns are the best."

"American westerns with John Wayne," Heinz agreed. He pointed an index finger like it was a pistol, and pretended to shoot his friend. "Take that you red-skinned savage!"

Erich staggered and fell against the wall of a nearby building in mock death. When Heinz offered his hand to help him up, Erich twisted around and put him in a head-lock. After a few minutes of friendly wrestling, Heinz cried uncle and they started toward home once again, talking and laughing as they went.

Suddenly, Erich stopped and grabbed Heinz's shoulder. "Do you hear that?"

*Flag held high, ranks firmly closed,*
*SA marches with a quiet, firm step.*

Nearby, voices were raised in the Horst Wessel song.

"Shit!" Erich hissed in a low voice. "I hate that Nazi song." They could see the glow of the fires coming closer. People gathered in the street to watch. Others, in the buildings along the route, drew their curtains and quickly turned out the lights.

"The Brown Shirts must be having another torch parade."

"From the sound of it, there must be a hundred of them," Erich said.

The column of storm-troopers turned into the street, carrying Nazi flags high in front of them.

"What are we going to do?" Heinz looked at the crowd of people that now surrounded them. "There's nowhere to run."

Erich saw the fear in his friend's face as the rows of torches marched past them. He took a deep breath, swallowing the fear that hammered his chest, and nodded resolutely. "We stand here and try not to be noticed."

All around them the crowd stood rigid, arms stretched high above their heads, pointing to the sky. Voices shouted cheers into the night.

Sieg Heil! Sieg Heil! Heil Hitler!

Erich tugged Heinz's sleeve to get his attention, then jerked his head to the side street where there seemed to be a small opening in the crowd. Without a word, they worked their way through the mob, slowly, so as not to draw attention to themselves.

Just as they stepped into the street and thought they were home free, rough hands grabbed them from behind.

"What do you think you're doing, turning your back on the flag?" The swastika seemed to pulse on the Brown Shirt's arm, and his eyes gleamed in the torchlight. He whipped around, pushing the boys to face the line of troopers carrying the flags with the broken cross.

"You will salute your flag now…"

To Erich the world had suddenly gone silent. He heard nothing but the Brown Shirt's menacing words echoing in his head. He glanced at Heinz. Their eyes met for an instant, and he knew his friend would stand with him, no matter what happened.

"I won't," he said. "That isn't my flag."

"Not your flag?" the Brown Shirt said, in a deceptively calm voice of disbelief. Then he backhanded Erich across the face with his fist, and sent him sprawling in the street.

Erich struggled to his feet, tasting blood from a split lip. Another Brown Shirt had Heinz's arms pinned behind his back. Now Heinz looked more angry than scared, and that gave Erich the courage to act when the Brown shirt again asked, "Not your flag? What are you? A Bolshevik?"

"No, I am a German. Not a Nazi."

The Brown Shirt's anger was a living thing ablaze in the torchlight. He grabbed Erich by his collar and shouted into his face, "You will salute the flag!" Erich flinched as much from the man's fetid breath as from the noise.

He wiped the man's spittle off his face with one hand, his eyes never leaving his attacker's, and with a quiet firmness said, "I will not."

Suddenly, sound returned to the world around him. Utter chaos as fists pummeled his face and stomach. Somewhere behind him, Heinz shouted his name, only to be cut off with a scream. Then Erich was on the ground, curling into a ball as polished boots kicked him in the ribs. With each kick, they hurled obscenities down on him. Commie. Bolshevik. Unpatriotic piece of shit.

Erich didn't realize the beating had stopped until he heard the singing again. The hated Horst Wessel song began to fade as the parade continued along its route, and the crowd dispersed. Every inch of his body screamed with pain. He slowly lifted his head to see where Heinz was, but it was dark and his eyes were swollen to slits.

"Heinz?" His voice rasped painfully.

A low moan sounded off to his left.

"I'm coming, Heinz," he said, forcing himself onto his hands and knees. He crawled to the dark lump in the street that was his friend. When he reached him, he put a hand on his arm, but before he could say anything, Heinz screamed and Erich fell backward.

"They broke my arm," Heinz groaned. Then, after they'd both caught their breath, he added, "I guess we were the Indians this time."

Erich tried to smile, but it hurt too much. "We'll get them back at the Little Big Horn." He struggled to his feet, then helped Heinz up, taking care this time not to touch the broken arm. "Let's go home."

"God in heaven! What happened?" Erich's mother shrieked when she saw him standing in the doorway, bruised and covered with blood. She ran to help him as he staggered inside.

"Nazis." The word slurred through his swollen lips, and he winced in pain as she steered him toward his bedroom. Then his father was there too, and Erich sagged against him in relief. His brother and sister came out of the kitchen to see what the commotion was. His mother's voice was sharp and in control when she spoke.

"Greta, fetch hot water and towels. Herbert, run to Dr. Braun's house. Tell him to come right away. Go now! Run!"

Two hours later, the doctor had come and gone. Erich had two black eyes, a broken nose, and assorted cuts and bruises. The doctor thought he might have a cracked rib or two, and had tightly bound his rib cage with strips from one of his mother's old bed sheets.

His mother kissed him lightly on the forehead, and left the room to comfort his sister, who had been crying ever since she'd first seen him in the hallway. Now his father sat next to him on the edge of the bed, and even through his swollen eyelids Erich could see the concern on his face. There hadn't been time to fully explain what had happened; all his father knew was that his youngest son had been brutally beaten by the Nazis.

"The doctor says you'll live. Do you feel up to telling me what happened?"

Erich told his father everything. He watched the emotions play across his father's face as he listened: frustration, anger, pride, pain, and love. When he finished his story, his father sighed and took hold of his hand.

"What you did took a lot of courage, and I am very proud of you. But it was also very stupid. Two young boys against a mob!" He shook his head at this sign of insanity. "You're lucky you weren't killed. And what if they had hauled you away to their jail? You must think before you act, Erich, not only of yourself, but of your family.

"You know what happens to people who resist—they disappear and their loved ones pay the price. The Nazis rule with fear and fear is a powerful weapon. With fear a handful of madmen can rule the world. You must promise me that you won't do anything so foolish again." His father squeezed his hand, and Erich thought he suddenly looked very old.

"I didn't mean for it to happen, Papa. They were there before we realized it."

"I understand, but these are dangerous times and we must all be vigilant." Then a wistful smile softened his face. "You must take care, my son. I couldn't bear to lose you."

Tears burned at the back of Erich's eyes, but he wouldn't let them fall. "I promise to be more careful, Papa. And I'll do my best to keep out of the Nazis' way."

"Good," his father said, and kissed his forehead. "That's a good boy. Sleep now. You need your rest."

I will be careful, Erich thought. But I won't let the Nazis rule me with fear either. They will never make me Sieg Heil.

# Granny's Nickels

Eleanor turned over the "Come In-We're Open" sign in the front window of Granny's Nickels, and hummed a happy tune as she went about setting up the coffee-maker at the end of the counter. If her first week in business was any indicator, the little consignment store with its variety of crafts and collectibles was going to be a success. Her grandmother's old mason jar already held a dollar in nickels, which meant she'd rung up twenty sales in the past four days. Not bad, considering it wasn't even the height of the tourist season yet.

A bell tinkled over the door as a middle-aged couple entered the store. Eleanor smiled in greeting. "Welcome to Granny's Nickels. If you see anything that interests you, just ask."

The man wore an old-fashioned straw hat, blue-striped seersucker slacks and a white shirt. His expression said he'd rather be on the golf course than shopping with his wife. And it was obvious to Eleanor that the woman in the flowered sundress was his wife by the way she tugged the man's elbow, directing him from one display to another.

"There's fresh hazelnut coffee, if you like," Eleanor said to the man, while his wife cooed over a porcelain doll. "No charge.

Help yourself." She heard the man mumble something as he extricated himself from his wife's grasp and made a bee-line to the counter.

The man nodded his appreciation as he sipped the coffee. "I don't usually go for the fancy stuff, but this is good."

"Thanks. I think it's grinding the beans fresh that makes all the difference," Eleanor said.

"I hate shopping," the man confided. "Especially for this frou-frou stuff. No offense."

Eleanor smiled. "None taken."

"Marilyn loves it though. When she noticed you were open…." The man sighed, then glanced over at his wife who was studying a table of handmade quilts. "She'll be at it forever."

"Well, there's plenty of coffee…and a restroom in back, if you need it," Eleanor winked mischievously.

"Thanks." The man turned and leaned against the counter, surveying the shop. "I must admit, this is a nice place you've got here. Catchy name too. Where did Granny's Nickels come from?"

"Well, it's a long story, but the Reader's Digest condensed version is this. My grandmother was born in 1913, the first year they minted the old buffalo head nickels. My great-grand-father, having been a cowboy in his youth, said the Indian on the nickel reminded him of an old Cheyenne he once knew, and decided to start collecting the new nickels as a dowry for his new daughter. They stopped making buffalo head nickels in 1938, but my great-grandfather didn't stop collecting them, and when my grandmother married the jar had $500.00 in it."

"That was a lot of money in those days," the man said.

"It was," Eleanor agreed. "My grandmother kept the jar of nickels for a rainy day, as she used to say, and kept saving any buffalo head nickels she came across. When she passed away last year, she bequeathed the jar to me. The face value of those nickels was around $1000.00...."

The man whistled softly. "But the value to collectors was...."

"A whole lot more," Eleanor said, grinning. "Enough to let me start this business, which is a dream come true for me."

"That's a great story. You should have it printed and framed. Put it on the wall with your grandmother's jar next to it. Let customers see the legacy."

"I just might do that. In fact, I've already decided to continue her tradition." Eleanor pointed to the mason jar with its dollar in nickels behind the counter. "For every sale, I put in a nickel. When it's full, I plan on donating the money to charity."

The man turned and called out to his wife, "Hey Honey, forget what I said about window-shopping. Buy whatever you like."

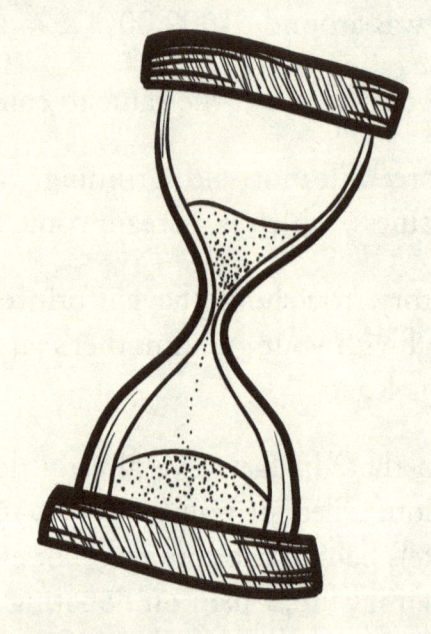

# Johnny Come Lately

Johnny Toad woke up with his head pounding and his mouth tasting like chalk. The realization hit him that he was lying spread-eagle on his stomach, clinging to something smooth and shiny about three feet above the ground. As he lifted his head to see where he was, Johnny found himself lying on top of a juice vending machine that had toppled over onto its side. And he was stark naked. Worse than that, he could feel his privates resting snugly in the slot that dispensed the juice. His aching head slammed back down on the machine. What the hell had happened?

He remembered stopping at the gas station late last night, only to find it locked up tight. The deserted stretch of road ahead gave no promise of other rest stops, so he decided to wait until morning when the station opened to fill up the empty gas tank rather than taking the chance of being stranded out in nowhere-land.

He still had two days before he had to meet the rest of his band in Lubbock. Pulling out his guitar, he sat on the hood of the red Chevy, grinding out all the old hits he and the band churned out night after night. "Toad and The Warts" had a string of hits back in the late '70s, and that's all that anyone wanted to hear anymore. Everyone wanted to walk down memory lane. Everyone except Johnny.

He remembered getting the bottle of Stoli from the trunk and he remembered using all his loose change to get cranberry juice from the vending machine. After that, everything got hazy. There was a fight with the machine when it wouldn't take his dollar bill. When it finally accepted his crumpled dollar, it stiffed him on his drink and he flew into a rage. He stepped back a few paces, then tackled the machine like a line backer, tumbling over along with it. After that, everything was a blank. Where the hell were his clothes? And how did he get naked in the first place?

"Mister, you're under arrest," a voice boomed from behind him.

"Damn," Johnny swore under his breath. "Officer, I can explain...."

"No need to explain. Being found drunk, naked, and apparently fornicatin' with a juice machine, is reason enough to lock you up in these parts. Not to mention, vandalizing private property. Looks to me like you're old enough to know better."

"But officer, you don't understand. I was waiting for the station to open...I've gotta get to Lubbock. Me and my band have got a gig tomorrow...."

"Guess you'll have to use your phone call to tell 'em you're not gonna make it," said the burly police officer. "Hey Virgil, bring me a blanket to cover this guy, will ya? Oh yeah, and by the looks of it, we'll need some WD-40 to get him loose from this machine too."

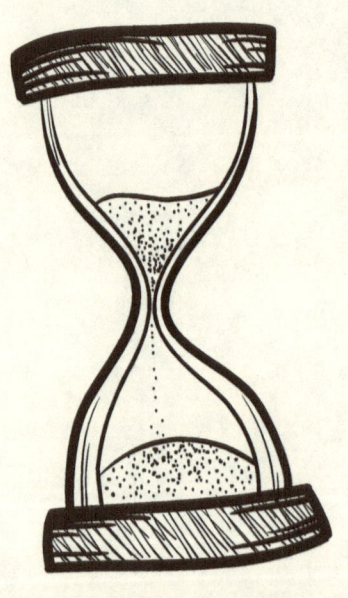

# Happy Birthday, Sister Mary Agnes!

She sat in the wheelchair with balloons tethered to its handles. There weren't one hundred of them, of course; a hundred of them might have lifted the chair and its pencil-thin inhabitant from the ground. No, the other nuns believed in miracles and weren't taking any chances with Sister Mary Agnes.

Sister Mary Agnes heard the susurrus of rubber against rubber as the balloons jiggled on their strings. She couldn't see any of this, of course. She hadn't been able to see anything since she was four years old, when a stray ember from the fireplace set fire to the flannel blanket she'd been wrapped in. They said it was a miracle she survived and a blessing she was blind. At least she didn't have to see her scar-covered body. Married to Christ, no one else would have to either. To say she hadn't been able to see anything wasn't really accurate. Over the years she'd had visions, portents of things to come, some good, some tragic. To her way of thinking, sight was overrated as senses went. She much preferred taste and touch, come to that.

All the sisters were gathered in the hall to celebrate Mary Agnes's birthday. In her mind's eye, she saw them all as they surrounded her, their angelic voices lifted in "Happy Birthday."

"A special treat for such a special occasion," Mother Superior said. "The Monsignor sent over a bottle of champagne to celebrate this happy day."

Mary Agnes heard the cork pop and the fizz as the glasses were filled. She felt plump fingers put a glass in her hand.

"Thank you, Sister Bernadette." She drank the whole glass in one gulp, burped loudly, then held out the empty glass. "More please, Sister."

Soft titters of laughter surrounded her and she smiled. People forgave a multitude of sins when you were as old as she was; she expected the same from the Lord when the time came. She had frightened enough people with her visions; she was glad she could bring them joy too. Thank heaven old age was good for something other than being wheeled into Mass and asking God when she could expect to see Him. She had a few questions she wanted to ask.

Roses. Suddenly, the room filled with roses. Red roses in brilliant contrast to the black and white habits. Their cloying perfume filled her nose and lungs and she sneezed.

"God bless you," the sisters chorused.

"I'm allergic to roses," Mary Agnes said, between sneezes. "Who brought the roses and why so many of them?"

Mother Superior took the empty wine glass that threatened to fall from Mary Agnes's grasp. "It's all right, Sister." She patted Mary Agnes's hand, attempting to placate, but the old nun would have none of Mother's condescension.

"I'm not senile," she said, annoyed. "I'm not imagining the roses. They are here. Hundreds of them. I can smell them. I can see them. I don't know what they mean, but they're there!"

She sneezed again, as if in punctuation.

Then, as suddenly as they had appeared, the roses were gone. Mary Agnes stopped sneezing and cocked her head to listen. The room was quiet, empty. The sisters were gone too.

Bright light surrounded her. If I could see, she thought, that would probably blind me. Out of the light she sensed hands reaching for hers, helping her rise from her chair. Then she was standing on her own, stronger than she'd been for many years. And suddenly, Mary Agnes knew where she was and what had happened.

She stood tall and spoke with confidence. "It's about time. I've got some questions to ask you."

"Ask what you will," came the voice, gentle and kind.

"If you knew I was allergic, why did you send the roses?"

Mary Agnes pulled a handkerchief from her sleeve, blew her nose loudly, and waited as her Lord's laughter washed over her.

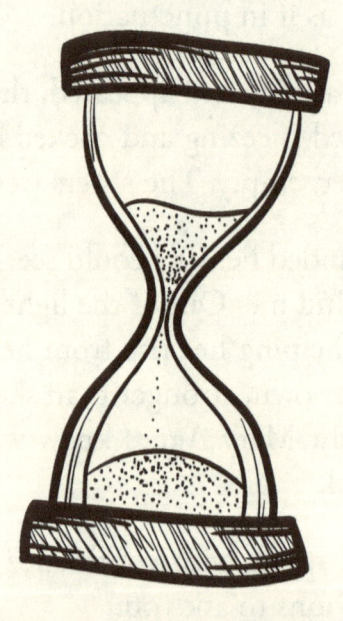

# One More Cat

P olice officer Henry Johnson could hear the cats meowing from outside the apartment door. Not only could he hear them, he could smell them, along with something else, something nastier than an unattended litter box. After nineteen years on the force, he knew in his gut this wasn't going to be pretty.

Emily Stein, his partner for the past three years, sensed it too. She wrinkled her nose and let out a sound of disgust. "Oh man, it smells like something's dead in there."

"That's what I think," said the little man with a pot-belly and bald head who stood behind the two police officers. "That's why I called you guys. You want I should open the door? I got a key to all the apartments in case of emergencies, but with the stink coming out of there, I was afraid of what I might find."

Henry rapped on the door, three hard knocks. "Mrs. Fitzpatrick? It's the police, ma'am. Are you all right?"

The meowing grew louder, and at least one of the cats was scratching the door from the other side. Henry knocked again, but no human response was forthcoming. On the off chance that the old woman wasn't beyond help, he thought it best to warn her about their next move.

"Mrs. Fitzpatrick? Don't be scared. We're going to help you. Mr. Nunez is going to use his pass key."

Henry stepped back and let the superintendent open the door. Two things happened simultaneously: a blur of cats raced out the door so fast they almost knocked the super over, and the three human beings standing in the hall all took an involuntary step backward as the stench rolled over them like a wave.

"I'm gonna be sick." Mr. Nunez gagged, and ran down the hall, presumably to his own apartment.

Officer Stein had covered her nose and mouth with one hand, her eyes watered from the acrid odor coming from the other side of the door. She clearly didn't want to go in there. Henry didn't blame her.

"It's all right, Em. I'll go in and see what's what." He stepped closer to the door, stopping when he was near enough to see inside. He sighed deeply. Over his shoulder, he said, "Call the ME's office. Better call the ASPCA too."

There were cats everywhere, and it seemed like the old lady had taken good care of them before she died. At least they'd been fed regularly. By the time the medical examiner got there, Henry had counted fourteen of them, not including the ones who had run out the door. Some of them of them looked wide-eyed and scared, but others seemed merely annoyed, as if having their human die without notice was a terrible inconvenience and how dare she!

One particular cat drew Henry's attention. It looked as though Mrs. Fitzpatrick had died in her rocking chair while watching television. The cat, a gray tabby, lay curled up in the old woman's lap, purring loudly. Henry moved closer to pick the cat up, being careful not to disturb anything else in the process.

"Well, I'll be damned. Will you look at that?"

"What is it?" Officer Stein asked, poking her head into the room from her place at the door.

"This cat's got six legs." He hadn't noticed anything odd about the animal at first, until it started to stretch, kneading its front paws on the old woman's lap and letting the rear paws extend behind him. That was when Henry saw the extra set of legs dangling from either side of the cat's bushy tail. The cat leapt to the floor with natural feline grace, despite the extra appendages dragging behind it.

Everyone turned to look at the oddity. All of them agreed they'd never seen anything like it. Dead bodies, while not exactly thick on the ground, weren't uncommon, but six-legged cats—now that was something else.

Henry picked up the cat, not caring about the hair sticking to his dark blue uniform, and started rubbing behind its ear. The cat moved its head, trying to guide Henry's fingers to the right spot. When he found it, the cat's purr rivaled that of his big cousins out in the jungle.

The guys from the animal shelter managed to capture and crate all the other cats, fifteen in all, not counting the six-legged tabby.

"They're in good shape," one of the men said, as he picked up one of the crates, preparing to bring it down to the truck. "There's a good chance we'll find homes for most of them. Probably not that one though—" he nodded toward the cat in Henry's arms. "Freak like that, they probably won't even wait the week before putting him to sleep."

"What if I take him?" Henry said. "Is that going to be a problem?"

The other fellow from the animal shelter smiled. "Not at all. Too many cats and not enough takers anyway. You'll be doing us a favor. Nobody likes to see them put down."

"Good." Henry checked his watch. His shift was over twenty minutes ago. He'd take the animal home on his way back to the station.

Officer Stein reached out to stroke the cat in her partner's arms, and looked at him dispassionately. "Another one, Henry? How many will this one make? Eight? Nine?"

"Ten. But who's counting?"

Emily Stein laughed. "I hope you've been buying stock in kitty litter."

"You don't mind taking care of the paperwork, do you, Em? After all, you do owe me one for letting you stay out in the hall…."

"I don't mind. But what about your other feline roommates? How are they gonna feel about this little guy?"

Henry smiled. "They'll take to this little fella just fine. They know there's plenty of room for all of them."

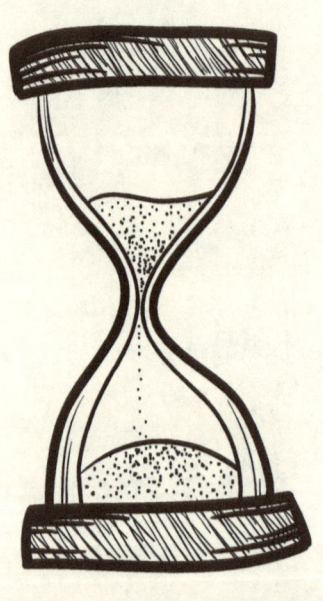

# Really, Mom…It's the Truth!

"**D**ANIEL RAYMOND LEWIS! What on earth went on here while I was gone? You're twelve years old! For heaven's sake, you should be able to watch your little brother while I go to the store without destroying the house. You better explain yourself, young man. And fast."

"It wasn't my fault, Mom. Honest."

"Don't even try to blame it on Paul. He's only three. He couldn't have made this much of a mess on his own—not if you were watching him like you were supposed to."

"I was watching him. He fell asleep when Mr. Rogers went to the Land of Make-Believe."

"Well, then we're back to it being your fault, aren't we, Daniel?"

"But I didn't do it! After Paul fell asleep, Dale came over with his new Ouija Board. You said it was okay for Dale to come over, remember?"

"I remember. Are you going to try to tell me Dale overturned all my potted plants and left corn chips, Coke bottles, and chicken bones all over the living room?"

"Of course not! Dale would never touch your plants."

"So, who did?"

"Zandor."

"Zandor? Who on earth is Zandor?"

"Oh, Zandor's not from Earth, Mom."

"He's not? You're not going to tell me he's a ghost you and Dale conjured up with the Ouija board, are you? I'm warning you, Daniel…."

"Don't be silly, Mom. There's no such things as ghosts. That's just kid's stuff."

"Well then…WHO IS ZANDOR?"

"He's the leader of an alien task force from the planet Tusxalo."

"Daniel, I'm rapidly losing patience…."

"Dale and I were just goofing around with the Ouija board. Then all of a sudden, the dial-thing started to hum really loud and moved to the letter 'Z,' then 'A,' then, 'N'…."

"Daniel…."

"Okay, okay. Sheesh! The board spelled out 'Zandor.' Dale was blaming me for moving the dial. I knew I didn't do it so I was blaming him. We headed to the kitchen to get some Cokes. All of a sudden, the whole room was filled with this really bright light. I mean, even sunglasses wouldn't have helped much to dim it. Then POOF, there's Zandor in the middle of the kitchen. He was huge—bigger than the refrigerator—and he had on this cool jumpsuit, kinda metallic blue with a funny looking helmet. It looked like a mini-flying saucer covered with tin foil."

"Oh, really."

"Really, Mom."

"And did Zandor say anything?"

"Not at first. He just looked at us real serious—like he was going to bite our heads off. Dale and I froze on the spot. I guess we were a little scared. Finally, he said, 'Are you the ones responsible for pulling me out of the stasis field?' His voice was really loud, like when Mr. Wilson yells at Dale and me for going into his flower beds. We just nodded."

"What did Zandor do then?"

"He looked around the room and said, 'I had no intention of making a rest stop on my way to Thalos IV, but since you forced me to, what have you got to eat?'"

"I suppose this is where the chicken and corn chips come in?"

"Yes, Ma'am. Since you were out grocery shopping, there wasn't much else to offer him."

"Want to tell me about the plants now?"

"Well, once we got the chicken and chips...and Cokes, of course, we all went to check on Paul. He was still sleeping... until Zandor tripped over the cat."

"Zandor tripped over Fluffy and spilled the bowl of corn chips. And that's how the plants got overturned? He fell into them?"

"No, he didn't fall into them."

"Then WHAT?"

"When he tripped over Fluffy, she clawed his leg. Zandor screamed. Talk about loud! Paul woke up and started crying until I gave him a couple of corn chips. I guess Fluffy was mad at Zandor for waking her up 'cause she started chasing him around the room and knocked over all your plants."

"So you're saying Fluffy destroyed my plants?"

"I know how much you love Fluffy, but it really was mostly her fault. Zandor was pretty happy once we fed him until Fluffy got in the way."

"And where is Zandor now, pray tell?"

"He said he had to get back on the road to Thalos IV. Some big doin's there. I think he might stop back on the return trip though."

"And what makes you say that, Daniel?"

"He forgot something."

"Oh? What's that?"

"His helmet. We used it for a corn chip bowl."

# Weddings Remembered

Kansas, June-1968

"Land sakes, Beth! If you don't just look the picture of your grandma on her wedding day, standing there in that self-same dress, well, I'll eat my hat. Josie, go get that photograph of you and Hal that sits on my dresser. I want Beth to see it."

Josie sighed. "Mama, I'm sixty-five years old. Will there ever be a day when I don't have to take orders from you?"

"On the day I meet my Maker, you can stop. Now hurry up. I want Beth to see that picture."

At ninety, the only concession to age that Great-Grandma Kit had made was her place in the wheelchair, forced on her by a broken hip two years earlier. And there she sat, nodding her approval, as she watched her great-granddaughter being fitted for her wedding gown.

"Oh, Grandma Kit, I just love this dress." Beth stretched out her arms and twirled around like a princess in a storybook, making the satin skirt billow at her feet and sending her long ebony curls flying.

Her mother, Susan, knelt at her side, and spoke through a mouthful of straight pins.

"Now Beth, hold still. I'll never get this hem straight if you keep moving." Beth made her best sad puppy-dog face and smiled as her mother tried not to laugh with the pins in her mouth.

Grandma Josie returned with the yellowed wedding photograph.

"You know, Mama, you're right. Beth does look a lot like I did back then."

"Of course, I'm right, Josie. I was there after all."

The old woman grabbed the bronze picture frame from her daughter, and wheeled herself closer to Beth.

"Looky here, Beth. If this picture was taken with one of those new cameras and you cut out Grandpa Hal's face, it could be you."

Beth grinned at the idea of cutting out Grandpa's face and replacing it with Paul's. She studied the aged photograph of her grandparents taken in the summer of 1920.

The dress had stood the test of time well. It was a simple but elegant design. Made of cream-colored satin with long mutton-chop sleeves, it had a sweetheart neckline and a narrow satin skirt that flared slightly from the waist to the floor. Grandma had kept it safe, packed away in the attic for almost fifty years.

Beth's mother hadn't worn the dress at her own wedding; her parents had eloped, much to the displeasure of the rest of the family. But Beth, the sixties' flower child, would wear the antique dress for her garden wedding. She not only loved the dress, but the history behind it, which she'd heard countless times throughout her childhood.

Her great-grandmother lifted her head and gazed into Beth's eyes. The old woman still had sparkle. Her life on the Kansas plains had been a rough one, but she'd met the challenge, and become a stronger person for having done so. That was what Beth wanted from life. That's why she and Paul would be leaving for the commune in the Colorado mountains after the wedding. They wanted to experience life as nature intended.

"I stitched that dress by hand, you know," Grandma Kit said. "No 'store bought' was good enough for my Josie." Josie smiled at her mother from her seat across the room. "I told Eustace, 'Our girl's gonna have the finest wedding dress this state's ever seen, so you just stop pitchin' a fit and order that satin, else you won't find me fit for living with, much less lovin'."

"Oh, Grandma! Did you really say that? I didn't think ladies talked that way back then," Beth teased.

"We didn't talk about private things in public, but when a man and wife are alone together there's not a thing they shouldn't be able to say to one another—especially if it's the truth. You bear that in mind once you and Paul are hitched.

"I made up my mind years before that if we ever had a daughter, she'd be married in the best, like my mama was. I didn't get to have a fancy wedding dress—Mama's was destroyed during the War when the Yankees torched the farm. Not that it wouldn't have mattered anyway." Grandma Kit brushed her hand in the air as if she were shooing flies. "My wedding didn't get much planning. Not like this affair you're having."

"Oh, Grandma, we're keeping it really simple. Paul and I want to get back to basics. That's why we're having the ceremony and reception in the garden."

"Balderdash! You don't know what simple is. Why when I arrived from back east, your great-grandpa didn't know when to expect me. He knew he'd sent for me, but travel being what it was at the time…. He got my telegraph the morning I was due to arrive. Laws! Was he surprised!" The old woman snorted laughter.

"It was late in the evening when I got off the train. Eustace collected me in an open-topped buggy and took me straight out to the justice of the peace's house. It wouldn't have been proper to go to our place first since we weren't married yet—not like young folks today with their free love and all." The old woman shook her head in disdain.

"Anyways, we were wed right in the middle of Justice Morgan's parlor, with his family, still in their nightclothes, as our witnesses. He said, 'Wilt thou, Katherine?' and I said, 'I will.' Then 'Wilt thou, Eustace?' and he said, 'I will.' He yawned and pronounced us man and wife. That was it. Then Eustace gave me the biggest kiss I'd ever had, right in front of everyone. Near buckled my knees, I can tell you." Grandma Kit laughed at her own tale. "Now that's a simple wedding."

"How romantic," Beth said, on a sigh.

Her mother had finished pinning the dress and was beginning to unbutton the back for her.

"You think it's romantic, Beth? Did Grandma Kit ever tell you what happened after the wedding?"

Susan turned to her grandmother. "Why don't you tell her that one? Maybe she won't be so excited about getting back to nature."

Beth frowned. She knew her mother wasn't happy about her plans to move to the commune.

"All right, Susan. No need to get persnickety. Beth's entitled to make her own decisions. You certainly did."

Susan scowled at her grandmother and Beth wished her parent's elopement wasn't still a bone of contention within the family.

Grandma Kit turned her attention back to Beth.

"I'll tell you this, child. What sounds romantic to you didn't seem so to me at the time. Life on the prairie wasn't anything like the life I'd known back east. Why there was nary a tree, for goodness sake! And most houses were made of sod and had dirt floors. Why, when I first laid eyes on the house that your great-grandfather made for us, I nearly turned tail for home.

"When Eustace drove the wagon back to our place after the wedding, he was all sweetness, telling me how fine it was that we were together again and how I was gonna learn to love the land as much as he did." The old woman's wrinkled mouth pursed in contemplation.

"Well, it must have been nearly midnight before he swung me down from the wagon and said, 'We're home, Kit.' I looked around and all I could see was a stovepipe chimney breathing smoke, sticking up from a little hillside.

"I asked him, 'Where is it?' He pointed to the hill where he'd made the dugout sod house. I didn't say a word. He took my hand and led me to the door, then lifted me over the threshold into the darkness. It was damp and smelled awful. Then he put me down and went to light a lamp. That's when I screamed."

Grandma Kit reached into the pocket of her sweater and pulled out a peppermint wrapped in cellophane. It took a moment before her gnarled hands were able to open the wrapper and pop the candy into her mouth.

"You can't leave me hanging there! What happened?" Beth said.

"Well," Kit said, sucking the peppermint into the side of her cheek. "Eustace jumped so high he nearly dropped the lantern and set the house on fire."

"But why did you scream?" Beth wanted to know. "What did you see?"

"A dead hog hanging from the ceiling. Eustace had butchered the animal earlier in the day, before he'd gotten my telegram. There wasn't a safe place to put it outside, where the scavengers wouldn't get it, so there it hung. I ran out the door and stood in the dark, already sour on this new home of mine.

"Naturally, I didn't go far. I had no place to go. My place was with my husband, for better or worse." Kit pointed a warning finger in Beth's face. "You just remember that when you take your vows. Make darn sure it's what you want before you get stuck with it."

"Yes, ma'am." Beth nodded. "But tell what happened next. What did you do?" She never tired of hearing Grandma Kit tell her prairie stories, every time hoping that this would be the time her grandmother would share some intimate detail she'd never mentioned before.

"As I recall, Eustace followed me out into the dark, all huffed up like I'd offended him somehow. He was a married man now and was hankering to enjoy some of the benefits of marriage, I reckon."

The old woman's face brightened as she replayed her memories; years seemed to fall off her time-worn visage and a mischievous grin tugged at her mouth.

"He tried to get me to come back into the house, but I told him I wasn't spending my wedding night with a dead hog. He went on about the whys of the situation, but I wasn't having none of it. Finally, he turned tail and went back into the dugout.

"Some time passed before he came back outside. 'It's taken care of Kit, now come back inside,' says he, like he's the man of the house and I'll do whatever he says. I reckon I was too tired to fight anymore so I followed him back in.

"Well, deary, your great-grandpa was no fool. He'd strung up a blanket across the room so I wouldn't have to look at that hog as I lay in our bed, and he'd thrown some onions in the fire to blot out the smell."

Kit began to laugh, loud and long. Her laughter was contagious and moments later, four generations of Parker women sat in the sewing room, laughing at their own beginnings.

When they finally calmed down, Beth sat at her great-grandmother's feet, resting her head in Kit's lap, while Beth's mother and grandmother went back to working on the dress alterations.

"Grandma?" Beth said, lifting her head to look into that beloved face. "That first night you and Grandpa spent in the dugout—was it wonderful?" she whispered.

Kit said nothing. For a moment, Beth thought she hadn't heard the question. Just when she was about to ask again, the old woman spoke in a voice so soft, Beth could barely hear her.

"Wonderful? No, child, it was better than that. It was worth it."

# Blooms From The Rain

The echoes of Lily's splashing and giggling floated down the hall from the bathroom, despite her grandmother's warning not to soak the floor.

"That child," Mabel said with a tired smile and a shake of her head. "Just goes to show I'm older than I thought."

"Oh Mom, you look younger every time I visit." Michael Warner sat at his mother's lace-covered dining room table sipping a cup of coffee. "Your hair even looks blonder than it did last week," he teased.

"That's gray, sonny boy. You gave me most of it. Lily's finishing the job."

Michael frowned into his cup and ran a hand through his hair. "I know it's not easy with Lily here all the time. I'm doing my best to convince her to come back to the house. It's just slow going."

"It's not all that hard, Michael—and you know I love Lily to pieces, but maybe it's not such a good idea to bring her back to the house. There are so many sad memories there. Maybe you should just sell it and start fresh elsewhere."

"I wish it was that easy. The neighborhood isn't choice any-more and people just aren't buying. Even if they were, look-ing out your front door at a pile of burnt rubble isn't a big inducement. Maybe if the damn town would get around to clearing it out…." Michael swallowed a sob. "God, I wish Heather was here."

Mabel patted his arm, then went to get Lily ready for bed. By the time his daughter bounded down the hall and into his lap, Michael had composed himself.

"Whose girl are you?" Michael asked, tickling her.

"Yours!" Lily squealed.

"It's time for bed, my little Lily-flower."

Lily clung to Michael like a monkey, her arms and legs wrapped around him as he stood and walked to the bedroom. He tucked her in, then sat on the edge of the bed. Thunder clapped in the distance and heavy rain hammered the panes of glass. Lily glanced nervously at the window.

"Do you have to go, Daddy? Can't you stay here with Grandma and me?"

"I wish I could, Lily, but someone's got to watch our house. Besides, it's too far for me to travel to work everyday. I'll be back again on Friday night. I promise."

"But Daddy, aren't you lonely there without me?"

Lonely. Out of the mouths of babes, he thought. He glanced at the picture on Lily's nightstand: Heather and Lily laughing in a field of wildflowers, so alike with their curly blonde hair and smiling blue eyes. Michael swallowed hard and turned back to his daughter.

"Sure, I'm lonely and I miss you like crazy. That's why I want you to come back home instead of staying here at Grandma's."

"But Daddy, I can't." Her voice changed to a pitiful whine. "When I see Doreen's house all burned up, it makes me want to cry. First Mommy died and then Doreen…." Lightning flashed and her little body shivered. When the thunder followed, she bolted into his arms and burst into tears. "Oh Daddy, I don't want you to die too."

Michael held her close, gently rocking as he stroked her back.

"I'm not going to die, Lily-flower. I'm not sick the way Mommy was."

"Doreen wasn't sick. What if the lightning hits our house while you're sleeping?"

How did you combat a child's logic in the face of unanswerable questions? Death had no logic. It made no sense. His beautiful wife was gone, ravaged by cancer. Little Doreen's life had been snuffed out in a fire that burned her house to the ground while her parents lay in a drugged stupor.

"That's not going to happen. God knows we need each other."

"We needed Mommy too."

Michael sighed. "I don't know all the answers. Maybe God took Doreen so Mommy could take care of her. You know Doreen's parents didn't treat her very nice. Maybe God thought it would be good for Mommy too, so she wouldn't miss us so much. After all, we still have each other."

Lily nodded and leaned back on her pillows. Michael kissed her forehead, relieved that his answer seemed to pacify her for the moment.

"Daddy? Will you tell me the Pinocchio story? Grandma doesn't tell it right. Please...."

With a lop-sided grin, Michael began their bedtime ritual. Using his index finger, he pretended Lily's nose grew a foot, then slowly shortened to normal size. As the two of them giggled, Michael kissed Lily again and tugged the blanket up to her neck. At the door, he turned once more before making the long trip home.

"Goodnight my little Lily-flower. I love you."

"I love you too, Daddy."

"Whose girl are you?"

"Yours!"

The two hour trip home from his mother's took nearly three that Sunday night. Traffic slowed to a crawl in the early spring storm. As the windshield wipers struggled to keep up with the steady downpour, Michael flipped on the radio hoping to brighten his sagging spirits. He missed Lily already. The days apart from her felt like years.

He understood his daughter's anxiety. His mother was right; the house represented all the sadness in Lily's short life. Sometimes the weight of that sadness dragged him down too, but the house also embodied the things in life that held meaning for him. He needed to find a way to help Lily remember the good things instead of the bad.

He turned off the main road and onto the side streets. He noticed, not for the first time, how much the area had deteriorated. More and more of the houses, in what was once a middle-class development, were in need of paint and yard work. Piles of garbage ransacked by stray animals cluttered the streets. Even the heavy rain didn't seem to daunt the gangs of teenagers who roamed the streets scattering a trail of empty beer bottles and cigarette butts.

Rounding the corner onto his block, the headlights swept over the pile of rubble across from his house that had once been a pretty little cottage with scalloped shingles and a white picket fence.

When the Skelniks had moved in a year ago, Lily was thrilled. She met Doreen, a skinny waif-like child her own age. Despite Doreen's shyness, the two girls became fast friends. Lily had been withdrawn since Heather's death the year before and Michael was happy to see his daughter smiling again.

Doreen's parents were another story. They rarely left the house; Michael assumed they were on welfare. The neighbors had called the police more than once, but that never stopped the screaming matches for long. He felt sorry for Doreen and encouraged Lily to invite her over whenever he could.

Looking at the charred remains of the Skelnik's house, memories of the flames lapping up the walls and firemen removing those three body-bags churned in his head. If he couldn't forget, how the hell could he expect Lily to?

Exhausted, with his feet dragging, he entered the empty house and hauled himself to bed. But sleep wouldn't come. He tossed and turned and hammered his pillow, sending vague prayers to heaven and Heather for a solution to his problem.

Early morning sunlight filled the kitchen. Another day to face alone, Michael thought as he leaned against the counter waiting for the coffee to finish brewing. If Heather was here, she'd be humming a cheerful tune while she made breakfast, brightening his day with her own brand of sunshine.

He grabbed a coffee mug from the cabinet; it had been one of Heather's favorites, with her name spelled out in yellow daisies. He smiled. Heather chose floral patterns for everything from the silverware to the wallpaper. Flowers. Always flowers.

Suddenly, he had an idea—or at least the beginning of one. Just maybe, Heather had sent an answer to his prayers after all. Feeling more hopeful than he had in months, Michael drank his coffee from the flowered cup, then drove to work formulating the details of his plan. If the town wouldn't clean up the eye sore, he would do it himself. He start with an internet search to see who owned the property, then see if he could get some kind of okay so he could get started right away. He'd be making them an offer they couldn't refuse; improving their property at no cost to them was bound to get their approval.

Michael grabbed a burger from a fast food joint on his way home, eating as he drove to save time. The days were getting longer and he didn't want to waste a moment of daylight. It was five o'clock when he pulled into his driveway. He went straight to the garage, grabbed some tools and headed across the street.

With a crowbar and ax, Michael pulled boards from the burnt house, and dragged them to the curb. The air was warm for late April. Before long his tee-shirt was damp with perspiration, and he was using the back of his forearm to wipe sweat from his forehead. He was tired, but kept chopping boards and pulling planks with an energy born of renewed hope. When darkness finally settled, he gathered up his tools and strolled across the street, whistling. He had made a start. It felt good to be doing something.

Each evening he worked clearing up the debris. One night, he noticed some of the neighborhood kids watching him. Egged on by his buddies, one of them came over to make inquiries.

"Hey man, what's doing?" a boy with green hair and a nose-ring asked. He glanced over his shoulder at his friends. Michael straightened and rested on his shovel.

"I think it's pretty obvious, don't you?"

"You gettin' paid to clean up that shit?"

"Nope."

The kid with the green hair snorted. "You shittin' me, right? Why you wanna do all that work for nothin'?"

"I'm doing it for me," Michael said. "I don't like looking out my window and seeing this mess." He nodded at the kid's buddies hanging in the background. "You and your friends are welcome to lend a hand. You could think of it as community service."

The green-haired kid snorted again. "Yeah, right. Like we're gonna bust our ass and not get paid. Get real, man."

Michael shook his head as he watched them walk away, listening to the echoes of their adolescent bravado. Once they were out of sight, he went home to have a beer and relax a little before bed. Tomorrow was Friday. He almost wished he didn't have to spend the weekend at his mother's. He hated to lose two full days of work on The Plan—he had begun to think of it in capital letters. He was anxious to see it finished. He wanted Lily home again.

Michael enjoyed the weekend with Lily. His spirits soared as he watched her roller skate down the sidewalk or jumping rope. His mother said he looked like the cat who swallowed the canary. Michael just smiled. The Plan would be his secret for a while longer. Sunday night came, time to say goodbye for another week. But soon, I won't have to leave her, Michael thought.

"Well, my little Lily-flower, it's time for me to head home." He tucked his daughter into bed, kissing her lightly on the forehead.

"Do you have to go, Daddy?" Lily fixed him with her wide-eyed gaze. "I miss you so much when you're gone."

"Now, Lily, we go through this every week. You know I have to go. Maybe soon you'll feel like coming with me. Until then, this is how it has to be."

Lily sighed. "Will you tell me the Pinocchio story before you go?"

"Don't I always?" Michael laughed and performed their bedtime ritual. With another hug and kiss, he headed for the door. "Whose girl are you?" he asked, grinning from the doorway.

"Yours, Daddy!"

By the time Michael got home, it was too dark to work on The Plan. The next morning dawned gray and ominous. The moment he stepped out his front door, the skies opened. The rain came in sheets, soaking him to the skin. He hoped it was only a cloudburst that would end quickly. He had a lot to do and working in the rain and muck wasn't going to make the job go any faster.

The rain didn't end quickly. The downpour continued throughout day. When he got home, Michael dragged himself to the kitchen and popped a frozen dinner in the microwave. He opened a beer and stared out his kitchen window, across the street. The pile of charred planks and rubbish at the curb grew bigger everyday. He realized he needed to call someone to get rid of it. The microwave beeped. He cursed softly, frustrated at the rain delaying his plans, then grabbed the phone book and searched for someone to haul away the debris.

Come morning, sunlight poured through his bedroom window. He jumped out of bed, his mood as bright as the day, knowing he'd be able to get back to work on The Plan. Minutes before he was due to leave for work, the phone rang.

"Daddy?"

"Hey, my little Lily-flower!" Michael said, with a smile in his voice. "What's up? I was just getting ready to leave for work."

"I had a bad dream last night. Grandma said I could call to make sure you're okay."

Michael ached hearing the worry in his daughter's voice. "I'm just fine. I'd say 'as right as rain' but we've had enough of that lately, don't you think?" He hoped his little joke would ease Lily's tension.

"Everything's a big puddle here. Grandma says I have to wear my rubber boots to school. I hate those boots. The boys always make fun of them."

"Don't worry about the boys. Boys are like that. I know, I used to be one once. You listen to grandma. We don't want you getting sick."

"Okay."

Michael glanced at the clock on the wall. "Look Lily, I've got to go or I'll be late for work. You have a good day at school, okay? And remember, I love you."

He hung up the phone and raced out the door. Halfway to work, he realized he'd forgotten the phone number of the hauling company on the kitchen table.

Michael backed the car into his driveway and sat dumbstruck for a full five minutes. He couldn't believe his eyes. He hadn't called the hauling company, yet the pile of debris was gone. On top of that, in the late afternoon sunshine, Michael noticed someone had been working on the site over the weekend. He knew it wasn't the town. He'd been trying to cut through their red tape for months with no success. He didn't think it was the kids who were hanging around. They'd made it clear they weren't working unless they got paid. Who then?

He got out of the car and walked across the street. On closer inspection, he realized the only things left on the property were the cement foundation and the few bushes lining the dilapidated fence.

"Looks a lot better, don't it?"

Michael whipped around, startled by the heavily accented voice of the man standing beside him. The man was short and sturdy looking, probably in his sixties. When Michael didn't answer immediately, the man offered his hand and said, "I don't think we met before. I'm Mancini—Vincenzo Mancini—but my wife and my friends, they call me Vinny."

Michael shook Mancini's hand."Michael Warner." He smiled, still puzzled. "You wouldn't happen to know who cleaned up this mess, would you?"

Mancini laughed. "Sure, I would! My wife saw you working so hard and she said, 'Vinny, we gotta give that boy some help. It's our neighborhood too.' So this morning she called my son Gino. He owns a hauling company. She told him to come right over. And that boy, he still listens to his Mama."

Mancini laughed again. "We loaded all the garbage and he hauled it away. Sophia walked around picking up the little pieces. Looks pretty good, no?"

"It looks great, Mr. Mancini. I've been anxious to get this eyesore cleaned up."

"I told you—my friends call me Vinny," Mancini interrupted.

"Vinny," Michael corrected. "Thanks for your help. This means I can start the next step of The Plan sooner than I thought."

"You got a plan? More than just getting rid of all the burned garbage?"

"Well, yes. I wanted to pretty the place up for my daughter...."

"Is she the little angel with the blonde curls I used to see playing here all the time?" Michael jumped at the female voice joining them from behind. She turned to Mancini and started badgering him. "Vinny, did you tell him we wanted to help? Or have you just been standing around wasting time? Aren't you going to introduce me?"

"Michael Warner, this is my wife, Sophia."

"It's a pleasure," Michael said. "To answer your question, yes, Lily is the little girl with the blonde curls. She's been staying with her grandmother since the fire."

"Such a terrible thing for a little girl to see," Sophia said. "And so sad about the other little one."

"That's one of the reasons I want to fix this place up again. Doreen was Lily's best friend."

"Well, it looks a lot better but it still looks pretty bad. I think it's still gonna remind her of the fire," Sophia said, apologetically.

"Well, now that it's all cleared out, I can get started on the next step. I plan to fill the property with flowers. I want to turn it into a giant garden. I thought I might put a few park benches on the foundation and repaint the fence. Make it look like an entirely different place."

Mancini's eyes widened and he slapped Michael on the back. "You're in luck then, my friend. My nephew owns a nursery across town. We can get what you need wholesale—or better yet, the family discount!"

"You're kidding, right? I mean, this is just too good to be true."

"He's not kidding," Sophia said. "Come to our house. I'll make coffee. We'll make a list of what you need."

Mancini talked his nephew into roto-tilling the property, free of charge. Michael and the Mancinis toiled on the garden every day for the next two weeks. As they raked, planted and fertilized the soil, Michael's spirits soared. He felt sure it wouldn't be long before he'd be able to bring Lily home. The idea filled him with excitement and a little fear.

"Not much left to do now," Vinny said, after swallowing the last of his Chianti. They were just finishing the celebration supper Sophia had made. Vinny reached for the straw-covered bottle and poured himself another glass of wine. Michael refused the refill, covering his glass with his hand.

"No thanks, Vinny. I've had enough. Sophia, that was the best lasagna I've ever eaten. I'm so stuffed, I doubt I'll be able to sleep tonight." He rubbed his hands over his stomach. Michael thought a bloated stomach wouldn't be the only reason he wouldn't sleep.

"So when will you bring Lily home?" Sophia asked. She continued before Michael had a chance to answer. "What's the matter? Where's your smile? The garden is almost ready. Lily will be coming home soon. Why do you look like you swallowed a bad olive?'

Michael leaned forward and rested his arms on the table.

"I guess I'm scared that after all this, Lily still won't be happy here. What if it's all been for nothing?"

"You stop that right now, Michael. You got to think positive. We've been lucky with the weather. Everything's blooming. The place looks wonderful. Things couldn't be any better. Even that boy with the green hair helped paint the fence—and for nothing! If that wasn't a sign from God, I don't know what is. Lily will love it. And even if she doesn't, all the work won't be for nothing. You've made the neighborhood a better place for all of us."

Sophia walked over to Michael and hugged him. "You told me your wife gave you a sign. Believe it."

"You're right, Sophia. I told Lily I'd be there tomorrow instead of tonight like I usually am. The mention of a surprise pacified her a little. Before I go, I want to put the flower pots around the foundation. If I get to my mother's by noon, I should be able to have Lily back here by three. Hopefully, I won't have to make the return trip."

"You won't, Michael," Vinny said, walking him to the door. "Sophia's right. Everything's going to work out just fine."

Sunshine, freshly squeezed from a citrus sun, poured over the spring Saturday. With the windows open, the warm breeze filled the car. Lily bounced in the seat, pointing out funny license plates and chatting about the events of the week. When she finally begged him to tell her the surprise, Michael's stomach twisted in a knot, certain that The Plan was suddenly going to turn into The Disaster. In half an hour he'd know for sure. He'd better prepare her now. He swallowed hard and screwed up his courage.

"Well, my little Lily-flower… we're going home." He glanced over at Lily, trying to gauge her expression. She gasped, her eyes wide and disbelieving.

"Now don't get upset. There's something special I want you to see. I've been working real hard on it for the last few weeks. After you see it, I'll take you back to grandma's if that's what you want."

Lily didn't say a word. She sat with her arms folded across her chest and stared out the window. Michael's attention shifted between the road and his daughter. He watched her chewing the inside of her cheek and wondered what was going through her mind. Was he crazy to think The Plan was going to make a difference? Then he thought of his wife. Heather had sent him the sign.

The Plan would work. It had to.

When the car turned onto their street, Lily scrunched down in the seat, her eyes fixed on the floor. Michael pulled into the driveway and turned off the ignition. The two of them sat quietly for a few minutes.

"Come on, Lily," Michael said, softly.

"Please, Daddy. Don't make me." Michael's heart ached hearing his daughter's pitiful plea. He forced himself to be strong.

"Lily, you know I love you more than anything in this world. I would never do anything to hurt you."

When Lily finally looked at him, a halo of sunlight framed her face. Her blue eyes filled with pools of unspilled sadness but she took hold of his hand and slid out the car door. With her eyes glued to her shoes, Lily walked where Michael led, down the driveway and across the street. He squatted in front of her, then lifted her chin until she looked into his eyes.

"Whose girl are you, Lily?"

"Yours," she whispered.

"Then trust me." He slowly turned her to face her fear.

Lily stood stunned by the explosion of color confronting her. She stepped closer to the freshly painted fence, gently fingering a sign on the gate that read, "Garden of Happy Memories."

She turned to Michael with a questioning glance. And something more, Michael thought. Hope, maybe? He nodded, encouraging her to take the steps toward healing.

Lily opened the gate and slowly walked up the stone path, bordered with pansies and violets. Azalea bushes surrounded the foundation, their colors alternating, pink, magenta, and white. Lily looked past the foundation where the entire backyard had been turned into a sea of color. She breathed deeply, inhaling the sweet fragrance of memories.

She turned to face Michael, who had followed her inside the gate. Along the fence behind him were rose bushes and hydrangeas with round balls of blue flowers. Every foot of the property was filled with growing things.

Suddenly Lily smiled and Michael was reminded of the picture of mother and child laughing in the field of daisies. He smiled back, opening his arms wide. Lily raced forward, throwing herself into his embrace, her arms wrapped tightly around his neck.

"Oh Daddy, it's beautiful."

Michael carried her up the stone steps of the foundation and sat down on one of the benches. Between the benches were dozens of flower pots filled with lilies. His own precious Lily sat on his lap.

"So, what do you think?" he finally asked.

"Did you do this all by yourself?" Lily still sounded awestruck.

Michael chuckled. "Well, not all by myself. I had some help from the Mancinis. And a nice boy with green hair painted the fence. But I did most of it."

"Green hair? I'd like to meet him."

"Well, maybe you will, if you decide to come back home."

Michael held his breath, waiting. Lily considered her surroundings once more, then bit her lip and nodded. Michael hugged her, as his heart filled with joy.

"What made you think of doing this?" Lily asked after they had been sitting for a while, absorbing the sunshine, the flowers and the spring air.

"Mommy," Michael said, quietly.

"Mommy?"

"Yes. I remembered how much she loved flowers. Next to you and me, I think Mommy loved flowers better than anything. She even named you after one." Michael tweaked Lily's nose and grinned. "I thought a place full of flowers would bring her closer to us. Help us remember all the happy memories. Even when winter comes and we can't see the flowers, we'll know they're still here, sleeping underground till springtime."

"It's like there's a little bit of Mommy in every flower, isn't it, Daddy?"

"That's right," Michael said, moved by his daughter's wisdom. "And Mommy's love is always here, just like the flowers waiting for spring to bloom again."

# Sunny Side Up

"Can I get you some more coffee?" Dorothy Jane asked with a smile so bright, she should've offered sunglasses to go with it. She placed the plate of sunny side eggs and extra crisp bacon in front the stiff-jawed man, who moments before had been shouting at his wife about the data overage on their phone bill. The wife nodded meekly, embarrassed by her husband's outburst. The man just thrust his cup in Dorothy Jane's direction. She filled both cups, then moved on to her next customer, not letting the couple's sour disposition spoil her own good mood.

Dorothy Jane was a morning person, that was why she chose to work the breakfast shift at Mel's Coffee Shop. It certainly wasn't for the tips, which were notoriously slim, or the prospect of meeting other smiling faces. In her experience, people like herself, who enjoyed greeting each new day, were definitely in the minority. No, Dorothy Jane just enjoyed the simple pleasures in life, like watching the sun come up golden on the horizon, the jingle of the wind chimes when a customer entered, or the smell of warm cinnamon buns sending subliminal messages to "taste me." She tugged at the front of her uniform where the buttons strained against her bosom. Dorothy Jane was very susceptible to suggestion, especially when it came from a warm cinnamon bun.

This morning, black clouds blocked the sun and it seemed the good Lord was squeezing every drop of moisture from them that He could. In contrast to the dark day, the wind chimes tinkled brightly when the door opened and a gust of wind followed the new customer inside.

"Morning, Sam!" Dorothy Jane followed the man to his usual booth in the corner, taking a fresh pot of coffee with her. He was small and the rain slicked back his dark hair. When he sat down, his feet barely touched the floor. He had once told her he'd been a jockey in his youth, but to Dorothy Jane, he looked more like a troll some witch had conjured.

"Good morning to you, Sunshine. I'll have my usual cinnamon bun," Sam said. "That is, if you haven't eaten the last one yourself." He winked and sent Dorothy Jane a lopsided grin as he measured a third teaspoon of sugar into his coffee cup.

"Saved one special, just for you."

As she turned to get the bun, Dorothy Jane reached around and grabbed Sam's hand just as it was ready to pat her behind. "How many times have I warned you about those itchy fingers of yours? This isn't the produce section at the grocery store. Squeezing the melons is not allowed."

They both laughed. She served Sam his bun and went to the customer waiting at the register.

It was a game they played every morning. Harmless fun, quite acceptable to Dorothy Jane, though every now and then, a new waitress would demand how she could put up with the harassment, especially from such an ugly little man.

But Dorothy Jane didn't see Sam as an ugly little man, or look at the world the way most people did. As far as she was concerned, most things were ugly on the surface; you needed to get beyond that to see the beauty in everything. So even on the bleakest of days, Dorothy Jane was able to find some brightness.

Business was slow. The couple arguing over the phone bill paid the check and Dorothy Jane wasn't surprised to see they hadn't left a tip. She shrugged it off and cleared their table for the next, hopefully more generous, patron. With the coffee shop as empty as it was, Jeff, the short order cook motioned that he was stepping outside for a smoke. Dorothy hummed along with the piped in muzak as she wiped down the already clean counter top.

"Hey there, Sunshine! Why don't you join me in a cup of coffee?"

"Well, Sam, you might be small, but I don't think we'd both fit."

"Ha! That joke was new when Napoleon was a cadet. Stop being such a comedian and come sit with me. You're entitled to a break, aren't you?"

Dorothy Jane shrugged. "What the heck? It's not like I've got anyone else to wait on."

She poured herself a cup of coffee, then held up the pot to Sam. "You want a refill?"

"Nah, just bring your sweet self over here."

Sitting across from Sam, Dorothy Jane couldn't help think what an odd picture the two of them must make. She was a big woman, who looked even bigger with her too tight pink uniform and her bleached blonde hair teased up high on her head. She admitted to herself she probably wore too much makeup for a middle-aged woman, but she liked being colorful.

Sam, by comparison, was tiny. Though his body was well proportioned, he stood under five feet tall. In spite of his penchant for sweets, he didn't have an ounce of fat on him and he was always nicely dressed. In fact, it was only his face, a road map of wrinkles surrounding a prominent nose, that reminded her of the trolls she'd seen in picture books as a child. But when he smiled, she couldn't, for the life of her, imagine Sam being mean or threatening to eat little children.

"Pretty quiet in here today, eh, Sunshine?" He smiled and sipped his coffee.

"Yeah, it gets like that. When there's an unexpected cloudburst, people crowd in here in a hurry. But on a day like today, when the sun never had a chance to show its face, most folks never leave the house."

"What do you mean, 'the sun never had a chance to show its face?' The sun's sitting right across from me, shining like always."

Dorothy Jane smiled. "You are a sweet talker, Sam. I'll give you that."

"What else will you give me?" Sam asked, winking mischievously.

"Another cup of coffee?"

"Thought I told you to stop playing comedian," Sam said. His voice was soft, more serious than usual.

The rain pelted hard against the roof; it crackled like popcorn popping, drowning out the muzak. Alone in the empty coffee shop, the pair silently sipped their coffee. It was intimate. And unexpected.

"Want half of my cinnamon bun, Sunshine?"

"No thanks, Sam. You eat it. You're still a growing boy."

"I stopped growing a long time ago and 'boy' is hardly an apt description."

"Sorry, if I offended you. You know I was only kidding."

"I know. Your sense of humor is one of the things I like best about you. I just wish sometimes that we could have a serious conversation. Maybe get to know each other a little better."

Dorothy Jane just stared at him, not knowing what to say.

"What? No jokes? I guess your mind is racing a mile a minute trying to figure a way out of this one that won't cost you your tip, eh?"

Dorothy Jane frowned. What was he thinking?

"That's not it, Sam. I'm just surprised, that's all. We always joke around. I sort of take that for granted. I wasn't expecting serious conversation, that's all."

"Well, it might surprise you to know, I think serious thoughts all the time. In fact, quite a few of them are about you. I often wonder what you do when you're not here. If you have someone special in your life. That sort of thing."

"Really? That's quite a revelation. I guess it never occurred to me that my customers might give me much thought past whether I got their orders right."

"Why not? Don't you ever wonder about them?" Sam's gaze held hers. She knew he was asking about one very specific customer.

"Sure, I do. Especially the regulars."

The back door of the kitchen slammed and Jeff suddenly appeared over the counter ledge. Seeing no new customers or breakfast orders waiting, he went back outside for another cigarette.

The moment of intimacy was broken. Sam slid out of the booth; he pulled a five dollar bill out of his pocket and put it on the table. He stood next to the still-sitting Dorothy Jane; it was probably the only time he'd be taller than she was, and he pressed his advantage.

"Do you think you might consider having dinner with me sometime, Dorothy Jane?"

"You're serious, aren't you?" She was still a bit dazed by the morning's unexpected turn of events.

"Absolutely. So serious, I'll even spring for dessert." Sam was smiling now, that smile that melted away the goblins. "Just say when."

"No time like the present. How does tonight sound to you?"

"Perfect…just like you, Sunshine."

# Turn A Page

T he electronic chime echoed through the cavernous room. Charlene picked up the intercom.

"It is nine o'clock. The library is now closed. Please take your selections to the checkout desk. The library will reopen tomorrow morning at 10 AM. Have a good evening."

Her voice was husky for a woman, sultry. People were always surprised to hear it coming from her petite frame. Somehow, that voice called up visions of glamorous, long-legged starlets, not the short librarian with hair knotted in a bun and dark, owl-like eyes peering through horn-rimmed glasses.

Charlene straightened her desk, tucked a copy of Elizabethan poetry into her briefcase, and started for home. She smiled politely at Henry, the elderly security guard, as she passed through the double glass doors. Hurrying down the steps, she listened to the clicking of her high-heeled shoes against the marble. She loved that sound. The faster she walked the faster they clicked, and she always walked fast. If she moved quickly, people couldn't catch up to her. They couldn't get close. She imagined she was gone before they noticed she was there.

Quick-stepping her way down several city blocks, she reached the small bakery on the corner of Oak and Wendell. The bakery was closed but a dim light glowed within. Charlene rang the doorbell, making the buzzer play a little tune.

Within moments, a dwarfish old man in seersucker pants and a white, short-sleeved shirt opened the door. A pair of reading glasses on top of his bald head slipped when he looked up to welcome her. Charlene caught the glasses before they fell, folded them up and put them in his shirt pocket.

"Uncle Billy, one of these days you're going to break these things if you don't learn to put them away properly." Charlene gave her undersized uncle an over-sized hug as the two of them went inside the bakery.

"Yeah, and one of these days you're gonna fall off those high heels of yours. So I'll have broken glasses, and you'll have a broken leg. Who do you think gets the better deal?"

Uncle Billy walked behind the glass bakery counter. In the morning, it would be filled with luscious cakes, cookies, and pastries; the smell of fresh baked breads would make mouths water. For now, the shelves were empty except for a square white box. He grabbed the box by its string and handed it to Charlene.

"Happy Birthday to my favorite niece! Of course, you're the only niece who bothers with me, irritable old cuss that I am. Now open the box already and get on with it. Bakers get up early, you know. It's way past my bedtime." The grin on his face belied the tone of his voice.

Charlene opened the box. The birthday cake inside looked like a marble rectangle. Pink and red sugar roses detailed the edges of the cake, woven together by their stems, so realistic you had to wonder if you'd prick your finger on the thorns. How like Uncle Billy to include the thorns. Etched in the center, the words written in fine calligraphy, broke her heart.

Our two souls therefor, which are one, though I must
go, endure not yet a breach, but an expansion, like
gold to airy thinnes beat.—John Donne

Charlene's eyes filled with tears. Uncle Billy looked up at her with lips pursed; he nodded slightly.

"Uncle Billy," she said, barely choking out the words. "It's beautiful. I must be the luckiest girl alive," she added quickly, trying to pull herself together. "How many people can say they're related to a world class baker and scholar?" She smiled but it didn't quite reach her eyes. The quotation on the cake indicated the news from Uncle Billy's doctor wasn't good. It was his way of saying he didn't have much time left.

"Come on, girl. Let's eat this cake. The tea is already brewing in back. I've been reading a new book of poetry while I was waiting for you. Come have a look. We can have one of our famous 'literary chats' while we eat."

The pair moved into the back room apartment. They sat down to tea and cake as if this were no different than any other of Charlene's past twenty birthdays. She'd come to live with Uncle Billy after her parents died in an auto accident when she was twelve. Every year since, Uncle Billy had made her a special cake for just the two of them. They would sit together, sharing cake, discussing events and ideas, but most often returning to literature. Through books, she'd traveled everywhere she'd ever dreamed of going. An early introduction to the classics and the great philosophers had led her to the career she loved: working in the library, surrounded by books.

"Charlene," Uncle Billy said, startling her from the moment of reverie. "It's all right, you know. I've had a long life—and a good one, too. I wouldn't change things one lick, most especially the way we are together. If I had any children of my own, I'd want them to be exactly like you."

"Uncle Billy—"

"No, let me finish. I treasure every moment we've ever spent together and I know you do, too. That's important, because we don't remember days or years. It's moments in time that stick in our heads. But Charlene, I think I created a monster.

"You're a smart woman with a wonderful sense of humor. You're attractive, too, if you'd stop hiding behind that 'Madame Librarian' facade. You're so wrapped up in books, you scarcely take your nose out of them to really live. You spend all your time working at the library or at home reading more books. Life is meant to be shared. Do you have a single friend—other than me?"

"And what's wrong with you being my friend?" she asked defensively. "I couldn't ask for finer."

Uncle Billy shook his head. "Charlene, you're deliberately missing the point. We both know I'm not going to be here much longer. No sense beating around the bush. You need to have a real life. Let your hair down. Stop running away from life the way I've watched you race down the streets. Make something happen. Don't just observe from the sidelines. Write it down so you won't forget. I won't be happy if I look down from heaven to see you're an empty shell. You don't want me unhappy—I will haunt you...."

Charlene's eyes blurred with tears, but she forced a small smile. "I love you, Uncle Billy. I don't know what I'll do without you."

"You won't be without me. Remember—an expansion, not a breach. I'll always be with you. But you must make a new life for yourself." He smiled as he spoke, so unlike the irascible image the rest of the world saw.

"I'm not sure I know how to do that." Charlene wiped the tears and swallowed the lump in her throat.

"You're a bright girl. You'll figure it out." Uncle Billy winked impishly. "Now you'd better go home so I can get some sleep. I haven't quit the day job yet."

With a kiss and a hug and her leftover cake, Charlene left the bakery. Her brisk walk was nearly a run as she headed to the bus stop, but she knew there was no escaping the truth.

Within three months the bakery was closed for good. Uncle Billy was released from the hospital after a short stay, refusing to spend his last days smelling disinfectant and listening to the hum of machines keeping him alive. Charlene stopped every evening on her way home from work to see if there was anything he needed. Always he snapped in reply, "I want you to get a life for yourself. Stop spending all your free time here."

Each time, she would force a smile and say, "I'll have plenty of time for that later."

One autumn night, six months after her birthday, she sat quietly visiting with Uncle Billy yet again. He was even smaller now, the cancer having taken control of his body. Stubborn as always, he never let it control his mind; he faced the cancer the way he had faced life, head on and ready to do battle.

"Charlene, I want you to do something for me."

"Whatever you want, Uncle Billy. Name it." She looked at his face lined with silent agony. He reached out and took her hand. A wince of pain, gone in a heartbeat, flitted across his face from the effort.

"I want you to promise me something. When this is over, you'll go on with your life. You will not waste your time mourning for me." It was a command; his voice, suddenly strong, accepting no arguments.

"I promise to try. That's the best I can do right now." She leaned over and kissed her uncle's forehead. "I have some news that might cheer you up. I stopped at a travel agency on my way here. I'm thinking of taking a trip to England to see the place that spawned all those authors we love so much."

"Don't just think about it, Charlene. Do it!" He snapped at her in his frustration, then went on more composed. "There's something I want you to read at my funeral." He paused to take a slow deep breath. Charlene protested but he raised a hand to silence her. She would do this for him; they both knew it. It was senseless to argue the point, especially now, when it cost him so dearly. "Shakespeare's sonnet, number twenty-nine. You know the one I mean."

Charlene nodded and gently tucked the blankets around her uncle. She read aloud to him from the volume of poetry they'd begun earlier in the week until he fell asleep. He looked amazingly childlike as dreams overtook him; a peaceful calm spread across his face as though no pain touched him. With a light kiss, she left.

The next morning, the phone call came. She sat like a robot, mechanically listening to the hospice nurse tell her news that Uncle Billy had died sometime during the night. In a trance, she hung up the phone and put her desk in order, making sure the volume of Shakespeare's sonnets was in her briefcase before she left the library. After quick condolences from her supervisor, Charlene left the building. She barely noticed her heels clicking against the marble or Henry's wave goodbye as she passed his post by the door.

The autumn sun was bright as the breeze blew leaves into little swirling cyclones around the handful of mourners at the grave side. Charlene blinked and wiped the tears filling her eyes, tears brought on not solely by her grief, but irritated from the contact lenses she now wore. Wrapped tightly in her black wool coat, she tried to block out the chill seeping through her skin. Unaccustomed to wearing her hair unbound, she struggled to keep the loose tresses out of her eyes and mouth as the wind caught and whipped them in her face. The minister finished his eulogy and motioned for her to come forward. Clearing her throat, she opened a small book.

"My uncle asked me to read this sonnet at his funeral." She looked away for a moment to clear her eyes. A single sparrow soared through the chilled morning air, darting, swinging on the wind, flinging himself into each new challenge.

"My uncle," she continued softly, without taking her eyes from the sparrow, "once told me there were only three kindnesses we may grant the dead, and that we may know how well one was loved by which of the three we hold true." She took a deep, shuddering breath. "I will remember him. I will miss him sorely. I will never be the same for having known him."

Charlene palmed the little book with one hand, with the other she stilled the pages from the fall breeze. Her sensual voice warmed the crisp autumn air.

> When, in disgrace with fortune and men's eyes,
> I all alone beweep my outcast state,
> And trouble deaf heaven with my bootless cries,
> And look upon myself, and curse my fate,
> Wishing me like to one more rich in hope,
> Featured like him, like him with friends possessed,
> Desiring this man's art and that man's scope,
> With what I most enjoy contented least;
> Yet in these thoughts myself almost despising,
> Haply I think on thee—and then my state,
> Like to the lark at break of day arising
> From sullen earth, sings hymns at heaven's gate;

For thy sweet love remembered such wealth brings
That then I scorn to change my state with kings.

Charlene slowly raised her head as she closed the book. She quietly thanked each of the mourners as they voiced their sympathy one last time. Finally, she stood alone. There was no one left to hear her words, spoken softly, but with quiet determination. She pulled the wind-blown hair away from her lips, sniffing her runny nose.

"Uncle Billy, I promise now what I should have promised while you were alive. I'm going to live life. For a start, I booked that trip to England. I leave next week." She swallowed hard. "I wish you were going with me… but I guess in a way you are."

A small but genuine smile curled about her lips. "I've got to go now. As you know, I've got a lot of catching up to do."

She laid the slim volume of sonnets amid the flowers on the coffin. With her face upturned to the wind, Charlene strode toward her new life.

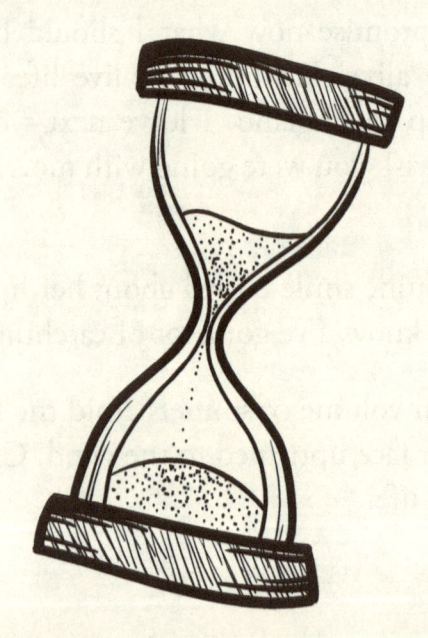

# Coming and Going

The waiter approaches a second time and noticing neither of the two pints of Guinness have been touched, flashes me a hopeful smile and asks if I've been stood up. I shake my head, throw another twenty dollar bill on the table, and tell him to keep them coming.

"Slainté," I whisper, clinking my glass against the unchaperoned one sitting across from me. The glass is soon as empty as my laugh. "That's dejá vu all over again."

It was five years ago, on a Monday afternoon, well past lunch, but too early for the happy hour crowd, when I first saw David. I watched him sitting in the corner booth with his elbows bent and the two day's stubble on his chin resting in the open palm of his hand. The Windsor knot of his conservative tie hung loosely around his neck; his gray suit, while good quality, needed pressing. Stringy black hair fell over his forehead, but not into his eyes, which appeared to be closed. A pinched expression crossed his face and I wondered if he was in pain or just asleep and in the throes of a bad dream.

Whatever the cause, I decided to find out for myself.

My running shoes squeaked on the varnished wood floor, the sound ending abruptly when I reached his booth. His head snapped up as if the sudden quiet startled him and I found myself gazing into eyes so filled with despair, a basset hound would look cheerful by comparison.

"Are you all right?"

He stared blankly at me. For half a moment, I didn't think he would answer, then slowly, almost imperceptibly, he nodded. "Yes. I'm fine, thank you." He had an Irish accent and he spoke with the gentlest voice I'd ever heard.

"You're not from around here," I said. "Let me buy you another drink." I motioned the waiter to bring another round and sat down in the seat opposite him before he could object.

"That's very kind of you," he said, sounding much too proper for his surroundings. He straightened in his seat and made a halfhearted effort to fix his tie. The waiter left two pints of Guinness on the table, took the twenty dollar bill I gave him, and winked appreciatively when I told him to keep the change.

"Jesse Collier," I said, reaching out to shake his hand.

He responded with a firm, business-like handshake. "David. David Leslie."

"Cheers." I raised my glass, expecting him to do the same.

He seemed far away, dazed, almost as if he'd forgotten I was there, and then as if something had pushed him from behind, he leaned forward and raised his glass.

"Slainté."

I sipped the dark stout and watched, transfixed, as he chugged his glass in one swallow, then wiped the foam from his upper lip with the back of his hand. The motion seemed incongruous to the proper, though disheveled looking, man before me.

"You drink that like you're a pro."

"A souvenir of my misspent youth," he said with a hollow laugh. "It's like riding a bicycle. You never forget how." He downed the rest in one gulp then gently set the glass on the table.

He didn't wipe his mouth this time. I stared at the bubbles clinging to the stubble around his pouting lips, wondering what his smile would look like. He rubbed his face with both hands; they slid up, as if trying to push both his hair and the frown lines off his forehead, failing miserably at both. The brown eyes were still clear; alcohol hadn't yet eased whatever pain lurked behind them.

I motioned to the waiter to bring another round. David reached for his wallet, but I stopped him. I handed the waiter another twenty. "Just keep 'em coming."

"Thank you," David said politely. "But you needn't spend all your money on me. I'm not destitute."

"I know, but the bar's empty and you look like you could use a friend."

"Do I?" His voice, though still gentle, was rich with sarcasm.

"Maybe I was wrong. If you want me to go…."

"No, don't!" He grabbed my wrist as if I'd been ready to bound out of the seat, then suddenly embarrassed by his outburst, he dropped it and took hold of his beer. "Sorry," he said, though I wasn't sure if he meant for grabbing me or his lack of emotional self-control. "Please. Forgive me."

I shrugged my shoulders and smiled. "Forget it."

We started talking the usual guy talk, careers and sports, and found we shared common interests in computers and soccer. The waiter dropped off the next round and we drank in companionable silence for a few moments. For the first time, I noticed the Claddaugh ring he wore on his left hand, a gold band with hands holding a heart.

"You married?" I asked. It seemed a logical progression of the conversation and yet, immediately I was sorry I'd asked. His jaw tightened, not in anger, but as if to bite back tears that were starting to rise.

"Unofficially," he said, once again chugging most of the fresh stout in one swallow. I drank slowly, unsure of what to say next.

"Look, David, do you want to talk about it? Did you two break up?"

"Mark's dead," he said flatly. "I buried him two days ago."

It was my turn to apologize, but what could I say? I'd been there. Hell, we've all been there and there's not a damn thing anyone can say to ease that pain. The alcohol must've finally hit him, because suddenly he started gushing; words and tears poured out in a flood.

"We were together for six years. I loved him. Everything about him, inside and out. Even when he was lying in that hospital bed, scarcely more than a skeleton, with tubes coming out everywhere, he was beautiful to me and I loved him. Even when I was angry because he was leaving me behind, I loved him...."

And then there were no more words, only the muffled, rasping sobs as he hid his face in his hands once more. I moved to his side of the booth, put my arms around him, and let him cry himself out.

I've sat here all afternoon, hidden in the darkness, reliving that day, guzzling Guinness and crying my eyes out. The only difference is David's not here and there's no one to hold me.

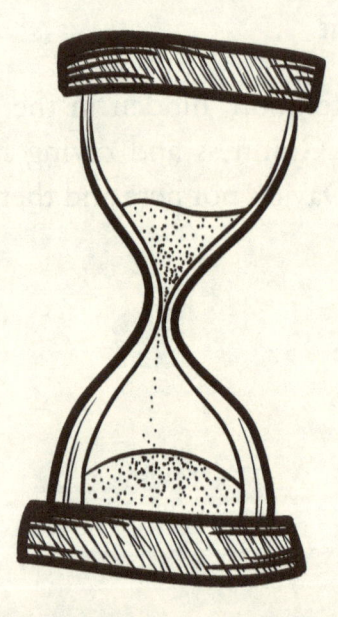

# The Devil Hath Charms

I lose things. My keys, my glasses, my job, my spouse, my child. My mind.

That's not the right order, of course. I started losing my mind somewhere between my glasses and my job. My husband escaped with my son not long after that. I don't blame him for going. In fact, I'm glad he did it. They're safe now. At least I hope they are.

Not that I'd ever hurt them. I love them with all my heart, which is why I'm not angry at Jim. He had to keep Billy safe. It's not me I'm worried about. It's the devil.

I know what you're thinking. She really is crazy. I think so too. I mean, no one in their right mind believes the devil is real. They believe there's evil in the world, but the guy with the red tail and horns, who instigates it and barters for souls, well, that's just fairy tale stuff, right? What they tell you when you're little to scare you into being good.

That's what I thought too, until I started to see him.

The first time I was walking in the woods behind our house. We have a big piece of property; the house and backyard sit on one acre, but there are ten acres of woodland behind that, with a small stream running along the far side where the property ends. I've always loved walking there. It's so peaceful and pretty. Spring and fall are my favorite times because of the colors, but summer and winter are lovely too. I taught Billy how to catch frogs and salamanders down by the stream.

But that first time I was alone. It wasn't quite spring; the trees hadn't even begun to bud. The air felt like it might rain, but I'd just had a big blow-out with Jim over finances and I wanted to be by myself for a while. I was pretty deep into the woods when I noticed a column of sunshine drifting between the trees, the way it always looks in the movies, almost like you'd expect to hear a choir of angels or the voice of God.

I remember wishing I had a camera with me, because it really was beautiful. Since I didn't, I decided to take a closer look. I thought I might stand in that stream of light and let it wash over me like a shower, maybe it would clean my cluttered mind.

When I reached the place where the column of light touched the ground, I saw the most incredible thing. The section of earth where the light fell, a circle about ten feet in diameter, was covered with daffodils. It was the damnedest thing. Impossible, but there it was. I stood staring at the flowers for I don't know how long, but I turned when I saw movement, out of the corner of my eye.

A man stood leaning against one of the big oaks. He was tall, dressed in jeans and a green cable knit sweater that matched his eyes, and made them sparkle like emeralds. His dark hair fell over his collar, and when he smiled I thought my heart would stop. He was the most beautiful man I'd ever seen.

"Hello," he said, in a voice so soft and sexy it was a caress. I couldn't speak. I just stood there like an idiot.

He slowly stepped away from the tree, and came toward me. I wasn't afraid, but I couldn't seem to move. It was like I'd taken root.

He stopped in the middle of the daffodils, spreading his arms wide. "Aren't they lovely?"

I nodded. When I finally found my voice I started tossing questions at him like I was a reporter for USA Today.

"Who are you? What are you doing here? Where did you come from? How did these flowers get here?"

He laughed, a warm and inviting laugh that melted my insides.

"I'm Michael. I was walking in the woods. When I came upon this place, I decided to have my lunch." He pointed to a backpack he'd left by the tree. "Care to join me?"

I shook my head. "I don't think so." I turned to look back in the direction I'd come from. "I've got to get back to the house. My husband's going to wonder where I am."

He looked disappointed. "Are you sure? I've got more than enough for two...and it's such a beautiful place for a picnic, don't you think?"

"It is," I agreed. God help me, but I wanted to stay.

He opened the pack and pulled out a bottle of red wine, along with two glasses. He smiled like a magician preparing to pull a rabbit out of his hat, and produced a container filled with cubed pieces of cheese and slices of fruit. He reached in again, and brought out a loaf of bread.

"You see? Too much for just me. Won't you please...?"

I should have left right then. I should have told him he was on private property and he needed pack up his belongings and vacate the premises. I did neither of those things.

His eyes and his smile beckoned. I thought this was all so impossible; I must be dreaming, so why shouldn't I indulge in the fantasy a while longer.

We spent the rest of the afternoon picnicking in the woods, surrounded by daffodils. We talked for hours and it was all so innocent; he never even touched me. The column of sunlight began to fade.

"Wait till I tell Jim about this," I said. "He's never going to believe it. I mean, who would? The crocuses haven't even sprouted near the house, so how the devil could these daffodils be in bloom? But there they are."

"Don't tell him," he whispered. "Let it be our little secret."

I giggled. That's when I knew I'd had too much of that wine, and if I told Jim he not only wouldn't believe me, but he'd think I'd been doing something else with Michael all afternoon.

"All right," I said. "It'll be our little secret."

We parted and went our separate ways.

The next day, after Jim left for work and I'd put Billy on the school bus, I decided to go back into the woods to find the patch of daffodils. I wanted to know if the meeting with Michael actually happened or if it really had been nothing more than a vivid dream.

After walking for what seemed like forever, I spotted a hint of yellow poking out of the shadows and headed for it. The flowers were there. So was Michael.

"Did you camp out?" I asked, a half dozen emotions skittering through me at once. Surprise. Excitement. Elation. Not to mention foreboding, worry, and a hint of fear.

Michael just smiled. "I was hoping you'd come back. I have more food." He jiggled his backpack, the way you might wiggle a bone at a dog, trying to tempt me. It seemed odd, yet compulsively seductive at the same time. I stayed with him until I had to leave to get Billy off the bus.

Everyday for the next week was the same. Once I was alone, I'd walk to the woods to meet Michael, always devilishly handsome, and always waiting for me with his pack filled with culinary delicacies.

The following Saturday, Billy went to a birthday party, which left Jim and me on our own. I don't know what came over me, but I wanted to tell him about the daffodils blooming in the wood. It was just too amazing a thing not to share. I didn't think what might happen if Michael was there, but I suppose some part of me thought the miracle of the flowers would be enough of a distraction.

It took some convincing, but I managed to get Jim to come with me. By this time, I could find the place without hunting for it, and was tugging Jim's arm to hurry him along. When the yellow of the daffodils came into view, I ran ahead until I stood in their center, and with my face lifted joyfully toward the sky, began spinning like a top.

"What the hell are you doing, Eva?"

Jim's voice sounded so irritated, I stopped immediately and looked at him. His lips puckered like he'd eaten a lemon, and there were deep creases in his forehead. For a moment I thought Michael might have been there and that was why Jim looked so pissy, but there was no one there except us.

"I'm dancing in the flowers, of course. Aren't they just amazing?"

"What flowers? You're standing in a patch of dead leaves."

It was my turn to look irritated.

"Dead leaves?" I picked a daffodil and waved it under his nose. "Does this look like a dead leaf to you?"

"That's exactly what it looks like—because that's what it is."

I didn't know what to say. It wasn't like Jim to be contrary for no reason, so why was he acting like this?

"Eva, honey, are you all right?" His voice went all solicitous and he was looking at me as if I'd gone crazy.

"I'm fine," I shouted. "Just fine. Let's forget the whole thing." Then I turned and stomped off ahead of him toward the house.

Jim wanted to talk when we got home, but I let him know I wasn't speaking to him, so he skulked off to the den to watch TV. We didn't speak to each other for the rest of the weekend.

On Monday, I went back to the place in the woods. Michael was waiting for me.

"I brought Jim to see the flowers," I said, without preamble.

"I know."

"He denied they were there. Told me I was seeing things!"

"I told you not to tell him," Michael said.

I hated hearing I-told-you-so from him, so I went on the offensive. "If you'd been here, you could've backed me up."

He shrugged. "Perhaps." An odd expression came over his face, a cross between impatience and seduction. "Maybe we shouldn't meet here anymore." He leaned close, his green eyes mesmerizing, as he slowly ran a finger along my cheek and over my bottom lip.

"You are so pretty," he said. "So very, very pretty."

Then he kissed me. Instantly, we were swallowed up in the heat of it. If I'd ever been kissed like that before, I swear I don't remember it. It was white-hot and I burned everywhere he touched me. It was incredible. I still don't know how I got home afterward. I walked around in a dream.

I met Michael in the woods everyday. I couldn't help myself. We made love in the flowers for hours. I should've realized something was wrong when the flowers always seemed to spring back to life, but I didn't. An army could've marched across the stream and I wouldn't have noticed. Michael held all my attention.

One evening after dinner, Jim said we had to talk. He sent Billy to spend the night at his friend's house so we'd be alone. That's when he told me he thought I needed to see a doctor.

When I asked him why, he said he was worried about me. My boss had called him that morning to say he was sorry I was sick, but he needed to hire someone to take my place. Jim didn't know I hadn't been to work in three weeks, but said nothing to my boss.

He decided to come home early and find out what was going on. When I wasn't in the house, he headed back to the woods.

"I saw you, Eva. You were naked in the leaves, rolling around and thrusting like you where having sex with somebody who wasn't there. You scared the shit out of me. I didn't know what to do, so I left you there and came home."

I didn't know what to say. Jim wasn't lying; I could see that in his face. He hadn't seen the flowers and he hadn't seen Michael.

But I had. Every one of the five senses had been at work while I was with Michael. I had no explanation for what was happening.

So that's why I'm in this locked room. Michael still visits me everyday and brings flowers. We wait until they turn out the lights to make love. They still can't see him, but I can. His green eyes glow in the dark.

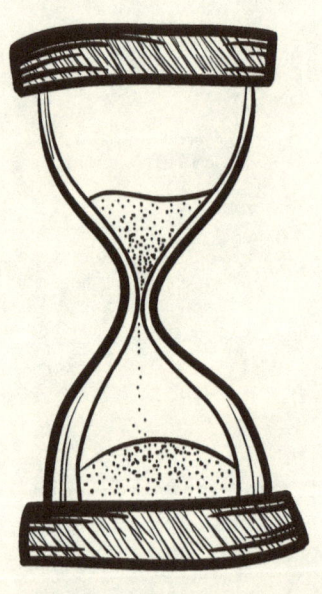

# Poetry on the Beach

Sam ambled down the empty beach, barefoot, with the cuffs of his slacks rolled up to his shins. His salt and pepper hair was mostly salt now and badly in need of a trim, and his unbuttoned shirt billowed in the breeze off the water like a flag run up a pole. He didn't care. He dropped his pack on the sand and sat down beside it, then he leaned back on his elbows with his knees up and stared at the endless sea and sky that stretched out before him.

Melanie would have called it a cotton candy sky with its rainbow of pinks and purples swirled amid the puffed cumulus clouds. She would have told him he was in a Prufrock state of mind and mocked his rolled trousers with lines from the poem. She would have asked him if he could hear the mermaids singing; he would have made a silly joke about preferring a woman with legs she could wrap around him, and then she would do exactly that, laughing all the time and making him soar right along with her. This beach was her place, their place. How many times had they strolled its length, watched its sunsets, made love in the dunes under the stars? More times than Sam could count. Not enough. Never enough.

But it had to be enough.

Sam sat straighter and wiped his eyes. Damn sand.

From out of nowhere, a dog sat down next to him. Whatever its heritage, its ancestors must have been big. It was gray and shaggy, and looked like a cross between a St. Bernard and a sheepdog. It cocked its head and looked at Sam with its tongue lolling to one side.

Sam scratched the dog behind the ear, noting it had no tags. "Where'd you come from, boy?" He glanced down the beach for the dog's owner, but saw no one. That was all right. He didn't want anyone intruding on what he came to do, but the dog would be okay. The dog wouldn't ask questions or spout meaningless cliches at him. The dog offered silent comfort just by being there.

The sun lowered on the horizon, casting diamonds on the water.

"I guess it's time."

The dog wagged its tail in acknowledgment. Sam unzipped his pack and pulled out a sealed plastic bowl and a sheet of paper, then stood up and walked to where the water kissed his toes with each breaking wave. The dog followed, its tail still wagging.

"This is what Melanie wanted," he said to the dog. "She chose the place and made me promise to read this as I let her go on the evening breeze."

The dog barked once, a short woofing sound, as if to say, "Then get on with it."

Sam swallowed hard and began to read.

> I am standing upon the seashore.
> A ship at my side spreads her white
> sails to the morning breeze and starts
> for the blue ocean.
> She is an object of beauty and strength.
> I stand and watch her until at length
> she hangs like a speck of white cloud
> just where the sea and sky come
> to mingle with each other.
> Then, someone at my side says;
> "There, she is gone!"
> "Gone where?"
> Gone from my sight. That is all.
> She is just as large in mast and hull
> and spar as she was when she left my side
> and she is just as able to bear her
> load of living freight to her destined port.
> Her diminished size is in me, not in her.
> And just at the moment when someone
> at my side says, "There, she is gone!"
> There are other eyes watching her coming,
> and other voices ready to take up the glad
> shout;
> "Here she comes!"
> And that is dying.

The last words broke on a sob. A gust of wind snatched the
paper out of Sam's hand and danced it over the water. The
dog took after it for a few steps, then stopped and simply

watched it fly. Sam opened the plastic bowl and set Melanie free in the wind, with the sand and the ocean she loved so much.

"Wait for me, sweetheart, and keep watching the horizon," he whispered, then turned to walk down the beach the way he'd come. The big gray dog trotted behind him.

Author's Note: The poem that Sam reads is by Henry Van Dyke, American short-story Writer, Poet and Essayist, 1852-1933

# Acknowledgments

I would like to give a special thank you to my daughter, Carrianne Palumbo, and my Cha-sister, Linda Grimes, for being the Beta Readers for this book. Their feedback, suggestions, and opinions were invaluable to me, and without them I'd probably still be trying to decide what order the stories should come in. If there are typos or other errors, the blame falls solely on me.

I'd also like to thank my publisher, Lisa Norman, who has been pushing me to put together a book of prose for years, and finally decided to focus her nagging, er, energy, on a collection of short stories rather than the unfinished novel that's sitting on my hard drive. She's the best and I appreciate her more than she will ever realize.

To my father, who I miss every day. He used to write stories when he was a boy, and though he didn't write them down, he used to make up little stories for me when I was a child. I like to think I got my "writing gene" from him. So much of both my poetry and prose has been inspired by him in one way or another. "Where Conscience Leads" in this anthology was based on an actual event in his life. I'm very grateful that he had a chance to read it, even more grateful that he was moved by it. Thank you, Dad, for everything.

And lastly, I'd like to thank everyone who's supported and encouraged me to keep writing and putting the words out there, be they poetry or prose. A writer without readers is still a writer, but it's so much more satisfying when you know someone is listening to what you have to say.

# About the Author

Elise Skidmore is an old soul whose love for prose was ironically rekindled by the digital revolution. A longstanding member of CompuServe's Writers Forum and Administrator of a private writers' group called SectionSixx, she delights in trading turns of phrase with literary compatriots worldwide.

A New Yorker by birth and by choice, Elise lives on the south shore of Long Island with her husband. While she misses her two grown children, she is quite proud of their success and independence.

Elise is also an *Epic eBook Award finalist* author for two of her three poetry anthologies, all of which contain her original photography in addition to the vivid tapestry of her words.

And while one may summarize Elise in any number of wonderful descriptors—mother, lover, bleeding-heart vigilante, free-thinker, troubadour, etc.—chief among them must always be *writer*.

# Other Books by
# Elise Skidmore